C000137834

Paid in Karma 3

Meesha

Lock Down Publications and Ca$h
Presents

Paid in Karma 3

A Novel by *Meesha*

Lock Down Publications
Po Box 944
Stockbridge, Ga 30281

Visit our website @
www.lockdownpublications.com

Copyright 2020 by Meesha
Paid in Karma 3

All rights reserved. No part of this book may be reproduced in any form or by electronic or mechanical means, including information storage and retrieval systems without permission in writing from the publisher, except by a reviewer who may quote brief passages in review.
First Edition June 2020
Printed in the United States of America

This is a work of fiction. Names, characters, places, and incidents either are products of the author's imagination or are used fictitiously. Any similarity to actual events or locales or persons, living or dead, is entirely coincidental.

Lock Down Publications
Like our page on Facebook: Lock Down Publications @
www.facebook.com/lockdownpublications.ldp
Cover design and layout by: **Dynasty Cover Me**
Book interior design by: **Shawn Walker**
Edited by: **Jill Duska**

Stay Connected with Us!

Text **LOCKDOWN** to 22828 to stay up-to-date with new releases, sneak peaks, contests and more...

Thank you.

Submission Guideline.

Submit the first three chapters of your completed manuscript to ldpsubmissions@gmail.com, subject line: Your book's title. The manuscript must be in a .doc file and sent as an attachment. Document should be in Times New Roman, double spaced and in size 12 font. Also, provide your synopsis and full contact information. If sending multiple submissions, they must each be in a separate email.

Have a story but no way to send it electronically? You can still submit to LDP/Ca$h Presents. Send in the first three chapters, written or typed, of your completed manuscript to:

LDP: Submissions Dept
Po Box 944
Stockbridge, Ga 30281

DO NOT send original manuscript. Must be a duplicate.

Provide your synopsis and a cover letter containing your full contact information.

Thanks for considering LDP and Ca$h Presents.

Dedication

This book is dedicated to Ladybug. It's been 5 years and you are still with me every step of the way during this journey. Losing you have been the worse pain I've ever endured, but you are still by my side pushing me every day. I know you are up above telling everyone in heaven how proud you are of me. I'm striving, Ladybug! The determination, motivation, and grind were instilled in me early on and I owe it all to you. I love and miss you. Keep protecting from afar and I will continue to make you proud. XOXO

Meesha

Chapter 1

Shanell

As I watched the blood flow quickly from Beverly's throat onto the floor, I grinned, slipping my hand into my leggings. The sight before me had me horny as fuck and I was determined to get my rocks off. I caressed my love bud ferociously with my fingers, which caused my breathing to labor. As I threw my head back and closed my eyes, a vision of Wes munching on my goods brought me to a heightened orgasm.

"Fuck!" I moaned as the creamy secretions oozed between my fingers. Placing my fingers in my mouth, I licked my sweetness from each one as I witnessed Beverly take her last breath. The nectar on my tongue made my nipples hard and I was for sure satisfied.

"Now you can mind your muthafuckin' business in peace, bitch!" I said, making my way out the back door. I could hear the sounds of sirens in the distance and knew it was time to get the fuck out of there. Kids laughing caught my attention.

"I'm having so much fun!"

Recognizing the voice as Sage's led me to the backyard next door. Sage and a few other kids were running around the yard playing football. He had the biggest smile on his face and I knew I had to act fast to get him away.

"Sage, play time is over. Tell your friends goodbye. We're going to see your mommy," I called out to him.

Sage stopped in his tracks and when he saw me, he ran as fast as his little feet could go and jumped into my arms.

"Auntie Nell!" he screamed, hugging my neck tightly. "Bye y'all, I'll be back to play later. I have to see my mommy!" Sage waved his little arm as I carried him, damn near running to the car I'd parked down the road.

Opening the door, I all but shoved him inside because the police had just pulled up in front of Beverly's house.

I ran to the driver's side and jumped in, pushing the start button on the rental. I backed onto the curb, made a U-turn, and went in the opposite direction of Beverly's house. It was a good thing I didn't have my car because it would've been easy to recognize if described by anyone. My car had started driving funny after I hit Bria's ass with it and I didn't want to take any chances with what I had planned.

"Auntie Nell, we have to go back. I need to tell Grandma Bev that I'm leaving," Sage said, poking his head between the seats.

"Sit your ass back and get in that seatbelt. We don't have to tell her shit!"

"But she's going to be worried about me. Mommy left me with her and she's going to think I got snatched by somebody."

"You did get snatched—by me! Now sit the fuck back like I told you!" I snapped.

"Why are you being so mean? I just wanted to tell Grandma Bev where I was going. I guess I'll just call her. Can I use your phone?" Sage asked.

"No, you can't use my phone! Now get in that damn seatbelt and don't let me tell you again!"

"I want my mommy!" Sage cried.

"If you drop a tear, I'm gon' whoop your ass! What have I told you about that crying shit? That's for punk muthafuckas! And let's get something clear right now. I'm your mother, not Bria!"

"You're not my mommy! You're Auntie Nell! Now take me to my mommy!" Sage screamed.

As bad as I wanted to slap the fuck out of him, I just kept driving. The shit I was on didn't have shit to do with what Sage's little ass was whining about. We had an eleven hour drive ahead of us because I had one more door to close before I came back to Chicago and ruined Wes once and for all.

Chapter 2

Wes

I thought about where Shanell could be and the fact that Bria had kept my son away from me. That shit pissed me off so badly because the bitch wasn't at her apartment when I got there. It was a damn shame I didn't know anything about the people Shanell interacted with after I was locked up. Curt couldn't tell me shit because she had killed his punk ass.

My mama wasn't answering her cell phone, but I knew she was probably downstairs with Sage and her phone was in her bedroom. I just wanted to spend time with my son and find many ways to make up for not being in his life for the past five fuckin' years. I signaled to get off at my exit, Dap did the same, and I was a few minutes from revealing the truth to my son and my mama.

As we turned onto my parents' street, I saw that there were over a dozen police cars lining the street. There was yellow tape blocking anyone from entering my parents' home. I could only drive so far up the street, so I threw the car in park and hopped out, running toward the house.

"Hold on, you can't go in there!" an officer yelled, stepping in front of me.

"Fuck you mean? That's my parents' house!" I said, pushing past him.

"I said you can't go in there!" the officer said, grabbing my arm.

"Get yo' muthafuckin' hands off him! We going in because my mama and my nephew in there!" Dap yelled, coming up behind us.

"Sir, this is an official crime scene and I can't let you go inside."

At that moment, a body was being brought out of the house covered in a body bag. My heart stopped for a minute and I pushed the officer and ran fast as I could toward the body. Three officers tackled me to the ground and I started swinging. I didn't give a fuck what happened to me. I had to see who the fuck was in that bag.

"Calm down, sir," an officer said after they had me pinned down to the ground. "Do you know who lives in this house?"

"My mama and son were in that house! Let me go so I can see if they are alright! Tell them not to put that body in that van! I need to see who's in there!" I screamed, trying to fight them off me.

"Let me the fuck go!" I heard Dap screaming, but I didn't know what was going on with him.

I was still being held down with force and the two fat fuckas wasn't letting up. My arms were going numb and I was getting madder with every minute that went by. "I need to see the damn body!" I screamed in the faces of the officers.

One of the officer's faces softened and he let me go completely and stood to his feet. "Pete, tell them to hold on. We can get identification for the victim."

"Are you sure?" he asked nervously.

"Yes. Only the face though."

Pete walked toward the stretcher and said something to the guys that were pushing it to the vehicle. One of them glanced over in my direction and nodded his head.

"Let them both up," the officer demanded.

I was let go immediately and I jumped up and slowly walked down the sidewalk. Dap fell in line with me and draped his arm over my shoulder. When we got to the stretcher, the body bag was opened slowly and my mama laid there motionless with blood on the side of her face. Falling to my knees, I wailed loudly. Dap pulled me up and grabbed me in his arms as we both cried like babies.

What the fuck happened? That was all that went through my mind. There was nobody that wanted my mama dead. She was well-liked in this neighborhood and everybody knew each other and looked out for one another. Shit didn't make sense at all to me. Sage came to mind and I broke away from Dap and headed for the house. Once again, I was stopped.

"You can't go in there, sir," an officer said shaking his head.

"Where is my son?" I screamed in his face with tears still flowing down my cheeks.

"There's no one else inside," he said.

I looked around in a daze and my eyes landed on the stretcher that was being loaded in the coroner's van. Dap was right there making sure my mother's body was placed inside securely. A hand was placed on my shoulder and I turned around, quickly coming face to face with one of the officers who pinned me to the ground.

"I'm Officer Stanford and first and foremost, I would like to extend my sincere condolences to you and your family. I was one of the first officers on the scene. I have a couple of questions to hopefully shine some light on this heinous crime."

"I don't have a problem answering any questions you may have, but I have to call my Pops and let him know what's going on," I said, taking my phone from my pocket.

"No problem, take your time, because we will be here for a while collecting evidence," Stanford said.

My hands were shaking uncontrollably as I attempted to call my Pops. Finally getting my fingers in order, I was able to pressed his name to place the call. The phone rang a couple times and when he answered, he was laughing with Bria. I hated to rain on their parade, but I had to deliver the news before he saw it on any news station.

"Hey, Wes," he said cheerfully. "Did y'all find her?"

I couldn't find my voice to save my life. This was by far the hardest thing I've ever had to do in my life. Truthfully, I didn't know how to tell him that the love of his life was gone forever. The mere thought of my mother being dead was breaking a nigga down. Being strong went out the window when I saw for myself that my mother was the person in the body bag.

"Wes! Wes, are you still there?" my Pops yelled into the phone.

My tongue felt heavy and I couldn't do anything but cry. Trying to suppress it the best I could without alarming him was hard as hell. Dap walked over and immediately grabbed the phone and hugged me like he was the big brother instead of the other way around. He put the phone up to his ear and exhaled before speaking.

"Old man, are you still at the hospital?" Dap asked. I didn't know what my father was saying on the other end, but I was glad my brother took over as my spokesperson because I wasn't going to be able to tell him about this one.

"He's right here, but there's an emergency and I need you to come home now," Dap paused. "I don't want to tell you over the phone, Pops. You need to come home," Dap said after a few seconds. "Since you insist," he said, taking a deep breath. "This is hard for me to tell you, but Beverly died, Pops. I don't know what happened and the police are here in the house."

Dap put the phone on speaker and my Pops was sobbing loudly. Hearing him cry caused me to cry. I had never witnessed my Pops shed a tear, so I knew he was hurt to the core.

"I'm on my way. Wait, where is Sage?" he asked.

"Sage wasn't in the house when the police arrived," I explained. "The officer is waiting to ask questions, so I'm going to find out as much as possible before you make it here. Drive safely, Pops, and I love you. We will get through this."

"I'm on my way, Wes, hold it together. Dap, you too, be strong," he said, disconnecting the call.

Officer Stanford walked over and it was time for us to find out what the fuck happened to my mama. I needed to figure out where the hell Sage was. There was no way my mama let him out of her sight with Bria being in the hospital. Shit wasn't making sense to me.

"Can the two of you come with me to the precinct?" he asked.

"Hell nawl! We gon' talk right here because my son is missing and my mama is dead! I know where she is, but we don't have a clue where Sage could be. You can tell me what the fuck happened to my mama for the time being though," I said, staring at his ass hard.

"A female called 911 dispatch and said there was an intruder in the home. She gave the address before the woman on the other end stopped responding. When I arrived on the scene, the front door was locked, but other officers were able to get in through the back. There weren't any signs of forced entry, so I'm assuming the victim knew her attacker," Stanford said, relaying what he was told and witnessed. "When we went inside the home, the victim was lying on the kitchen floor deceased from her injuries. The house was thor-

14

oughly searched and there was no one else in the house, so we secured the scene," he said, taking out a small notebook. "What is the victim's name?"

"Beverly King," I whispered. *Somebody killed my mother*, was the only thing on my mind.

"I'm sorry, I didn't hear you."

"Beverly King," I said a little louder.

"Did she live in the house alone?"

"No, my father, her husband, resides in the home with her," I choked out.

"What is your father's name and where can I find him?" Stanford asked.

"Weston King Sr., and he's on his way here. Don't even assume he had anything to do with this crime. One thing my father loved besides his kids was my mama! He was at the hospital with my sister and that's the only reason my son was here alone at the house with her."

When I mentioned Bria being at the hospital, I automatically thought about Shanell. The bitch came to this muthafucka and killed my mama to get back at me. There was no other explanation. I looked to my left and Dap had a weird expression on his face.

"I wasn't going to accuse your father, but I have to cover all bases. Everyone is a suspect until we can eliminate them. Anyone close to the victim is the first to be questioned, including the two of you. What are your names and relation to the victim?" Stanford asked.

"I'm Weston King Jr. and Beverly is my mama, like I stated numerous times in the past hour," I said, trying to be cooperative, but my patience was running thin.

Stanford moved his attention to Dap. The cop looked him up and down and stared longer at his diamond-encrusted Custom chain. The muthafucka was judging my brother off material shit. I bet he already had it in his mind that Dap was some type of drug dealer and that my mother's death was a hit or some shit.

15

"That muthafucka tight, ain't it?" Dap said, taking a step back. "Ask all your questions now and I will answer them truthfully. Don't categorize me prematurely," Dap sneered.

"Who are you and what is your relation to Mrs. King?" Stanford asked, peering at Dap.

"I'm Donovan King and Beverly is my stepmother. Now ask the question that's dancing off the tip of your tongue so we can focus on my family," Dap said, folding his arms over his chest.

"What is your job description?" Stanford asked boldly.

"I *own* Customs by Dap based in California and I just opened another location here in Chicago. No, I'm not a drug dealer, and if you would like to shop jewels, hit a nigga up," Dap said with a smile while handing the officer one of his business cards. "All black people aren't into illegal shit. I'm always looking for security. I may have a job for you," he smirked.

Reading over the card, the officer's face was beet red because Dap called him out on his bullshit. Stanford looked embarrassed and his fellow officers that were standing close by whispered amongst themselves. Investigators were busy walking in and out of the house with bags of evidence.

"Mr. King, I wasn't implying that you were into anything illegal—"

"Yeah, aight. What are you going to do far as my nephew? We don't know where Sage is and he was for sure here with Beverly this morning," Dap said, getting the focus off him and back on the problem at hand.

"We didn't see a child in the home, so we didn't know anything about him until you mentioned it. Do you have a picture of the child?"

"No, I don't," I replied. "I can get one. Hold on a sec." I went to my phone to text Bria for a pic, but the words of the cop stopped me midway.

"How is it that you don't have a picture of your son? That is very unusual for a father. If someone asked me to see any of my children, I could go right into my phone and produce plenty."

16

"What you won't do is try to discredit me as a father! I just learned he was my son today, smart ass! As of last night, he was introduced as my nephew."

I instantly got pissed because his bitch ass was acting as if I was a deadbeat nigga. Before I could say more, Miss Clara came walking toward us and she was crying. Rushing to meet her halfway, I opened my arms and she fell into them.

"Wes, oh my God, what happened?" she cried. "I saw the police, but I've been trying to find Sage!"

"You know about Sage, Miss Clara?" I asked, pushing her back gently so I could see her face.

"Yes. Beverly called asking if he could come over to play with the twins and I told her yes. When I went out to check on them, the boys said his aunt had come to pick him up so he could see his mother. I called Beverly, but she didn't answer, then I heard the sirens and all the police cars swarmed the block."

Officer Stanford walked up on us and cleared his throat. "Um, excuse me. I'm Officer Stanford and I overheard you talking about the boy."

"His name is Sage! Address him as such," I shot back at him.

"Who is this aunt you referenced? I need to know everything so we can find the boy—I mean, Sage."

"Lonnie, my grandson, said Sage called her Auntie Nell," Miss Clara said nervously. "I'm sorry, Wes, this is all my fault."

My hearing went out after Miss Clara mentioned Auntie Nell. My heart started beating loudly in my ears and everything else was heard as if I was underwater. The only thing I saw was everybody's mouth moving, but I couldn't hear shit. The bitch had my son and I was sure she killed my mama too.

"Wes!" Dap yelled, shaking me by the shoulders. "Stay with me, brah."

Blinking a couple times, I stared out into the street and spotted my father's car. The officer was looking at me weirdly and I didn't like that shit at all. He paced in front of me without saying a word.

Finally, he opened his mouth. "Mr. King, do you know the person that took your son?" Stanford asked.

I nodded my head. "Yes, she's my ex. I've been having many problems with Miss Jones in the past few months."

"What type of problems, Mr. King?" Stanford asked.

"Shanell has been making my life a living hell since I broke things off with her. We were in a relationship for years and I married another woman. She destroyed the apartment she lived in and cost me thousands of dollars in repairs. Shanell kidnapped my daughter from my wife's hospital room and hid her in a closet. She wasn't harmed, but the mere fact she got close to Faith scared the shit out of me," I explained. "Shanell also drugged and raped me. She captured it all on film and played it at my wife's baby shower. She sent a replica doll of my daughter to my home with a knife sticking out of the chest. Not only that, she admitted to murdering Curtis Miles at the gas station on 59th Street a week or so ago. Shanell also hit my sister with her car and that's the reason she's in the hospital now."

"Why isn't this Shanell person behind bars? All of those things are grounds for stalking, harassment, and assault with a deadly weapon," Stanford stated.

"I reported every incident besides the one about Curtis Miles because she just told me that last night. And that was before I found out she ran my sister over. I was told each and every time that I didn't have enough proof that Shanell was involved. Now that my mother has lost her life, and yes, I believe Shanell did it, the police see it the way I've seen it from the beginning."

"You muthafuckin' cops failed us! What the fuck do y'all get paid for? Because it's not to serve and protect!" Dap snapped. "It always comes down to somebody losing their life before any action takes place. It's bullshit, and this situation won't change the way shit is conducted for people like us!"

My father walked up to us on the front lawn, looking like he had aged a few years in a matter of an hour. "Tell me what's going on," he said as he stood in front of us.

"Who are you?" Stanford asked.

"I'm Weston Sr. Where's my wife? I want to see her."

"Mr. King, your wife has been taken to the morgue. You won't be able to see her until—"

"I want to see my wife now!" Pops yelled. "That bitch did this shit and I want you to know, she is dead when I find her. I will live the last days of my life in jail because she took the only woman I've ever loved from me!"

"Mr. King, none of that will be necessary. Leave everything to us, the police. The last thing you need to do is go to prison for taking the law into your own hands."

"Fuck the law! I'm taking full responsibility for my family because that's my job! Do your job and let me do mine! You heard what I said, and I'm standing on my shit! Find Shanell before I do, because the bitch is good as dead!"

My Pops was beyond mad and had every right. My mother was his world outside of us and we were all dying inside. Our days of being a happy family were cut short, and I didn't know how we would go forth after this tragedy.

Meesha

Chapter 3

Justice

"Waaa! Waaa!" Faith started screaming uncontrollably out of nowhere and I tried everything to calm her, but nothing worked. The bottle I made, she didn't want. I walked around bouncing her for fifteen minutes straight and that didn't work either. Faith's diaper was dry too so I decided to put on the Motown nursery rhymes Beverly had found to entertain her and she settled down by resting her head on my shoulder. My baby was sleeping in a matter of minutes and I was confused about the entire scenario that had played out.

As I placed Faith in her crib, I heard the alarm beep, alerting me that Wes was home. He had been gone all day and I didn't bother him because he and his family were dealing with Bria. As for me, I wasn't dealing with Wes' sister because of the bullshit she pulled with Shanell. They could forgive her, because that's what family did for one another, but I didn't have to do shit I didn't want to do. To prevent myself from beating her ass again, I'd just stay away from her.

I walked down the hall to our bedroom and sat on the foot of the bed and waited for Wes to come upstairs. After fifteen minutes of being alone and no sign of my husband, I got up and made my way downstairs to find him. The music coming from his man cave in the basement told me just where he was. As I slowly opened the door, the sound of Tupac's "Dear Mama" bounced off the walls.

And I appreciate, how you raised me
And all the extra love that you gave me
I wish I could take the pain away
If you make it through the night, there's a brighter day
Everything will be alright if you hold on
It's a struggle every day gotta roll on
And there's no way I can pay ya back
But my plan is to show you that I understand
You are appreciated.

As I made my way down the steps, the smell of marijuana hit me in the face. The aroma made me move faster. My husband was sitting at the bar with a blunt in his hand and tears running down his face. My heart crumbled. I'd never seen Wes shed a tear and the fact that he was smoking told me something bad had happened. My feet wouldn't move because he was staring right at me but in a sense, he wasn't seeing me. He reached for the half full Henny bottle and turned it up.

"Baby, what's the matter?" I asked, walking slowly in his direction.

Wes slammed the bottle down on the bar and instead of answering, he took a long toke from the blunt. The smoke came out of his nose and mouth as he took a tissue from the box and wiped the snot from his nose. Not wanting to rush him, I waited until he was ready to open up to me. Gathering his composure somewhat, Wes threw the tissue in the trash can and focused on me. Fresh tears welled in his eyes and my nose started tingling because I felt his pain, but didn't know the cause.

"She's gone, Justice!" he cried. "She didn't deserve that shit, man!" Wes hit the blunt deeply and held the smoke in as he placed it in the ashtray. He picked up a fresh wood and started filling it with weed.

"Who's gone? Bria? I thought her injuries wasn't serious." I didn't care for Bria, but I wouldn't wish death on her because I didn't like her. I'm not that damn insensitive.

"My—my—my mama," he broke down, grabbing the bottle and taking it to the head.

"Oh, maybe she just needed time away, babe. She'll start to miss Faith, and you know she can't stay away from her too long. Stop crying," I said, taking the bottle from him. "You've had enough of this."

"Justice, she's not coming back. She's dead! That bitch killed my mama!"

The words Wes revealed stabbed me in my chest and I felt faint. There was no way Beverly was gone forever. I was just at her house.

"Wait a minute, what do you mean Beverly's dead? And who the fuck is the bitch?" I asked, stepping away from him.

"I just came from the morgue with Pops and Dap. I wouldn't wish that shit on my worst enemy. Her throat was cut so fuckin' deep, I can't even describe what the hell I saw. All I know, when I catch up with Shanell, her muthafuckin' ass is dead! She killed my mama and took my son!"

I heard what Wes said but the last sentence stood out like a sore thumb. "Your son? Tell me everything, Wes, and don't leave anything out," I said, taking a seat on the barstool next to him.

Before he attempted to say anything, Wes lit the blunt he rolled and hit it hard. "When we were at the hospital checking on Bria, Dap was the first to arrive. Me and Pops walked in on their conversation and my sister has been keeping a serious secret from us all!" he cried. "Sage is my son, Justice. The reason Bria is lying in the hospital is because she went to see Shanell to let her know it was time to tell me about my son."

"I knew it! That boy looks just like you and the way she was avoiding the questions about his daddy brought further suspicions." I wasn't shocked about his revelation because I had a feeling something wasn't being told on Bria's end.

"Shanell didn't want Bria to say anything and tried to choke her out. Some type of way, Bria got away from her and ran after she dropped the keys to Pops' whip. Shanell ran Bria down with her car and left my sister for dead in a fuckin' alley!"

The tears were now gone and were replaced with pure anger. Wes' face contorted into something I hadn't seen before and it was like he was a different person altogether. The man I married wasn't present in my home.

"Then she took her ass to my mama's house and killed her! I'm going to tear this fuckin' city up until I find that bitch! Fuck my job, the police, and anyone that tries to stand in my way!" he yelled loudly. "Justice, I have hundreds of personal time off hours and I'm about to use them. This is a side of me that I never wanted you to see, but I have to handle this shit myself."

Wes put the blunt out and stood to his feet. He looked down at the khaki pants and polo shirt he wore and walked to the closet on the other side of the room. I didn't invade his privacy when it came to his space, so I had no idea that he had a whole wardrobe down in the man cave. I watched as he pulled the shirt over his head and stepped out of his pants. Wes then snatched a black sweat suit from a hanger and put it on.

"Baby, where are you going?" I asked, standing up.

"I need some air. Don't wait up for me," he said as he put on a fitted cap and turned it backwards. My husband transformed into a street nigga right before my eyes and my pussy thumped erratically. It had been years since I'd messed around with a thug and I thought I was over that shit when I married my successful husband. His phone rang on the bar and I looked down to see who was calling, and it was Dap.

"Answer that for me," Wes said as he pulled on his all-black Nikes.

"Hello," I said, doing as I was told.

"Hey, sis. Where's Wes?" Dap asked.

"He's right here. How are you, Dap?"

"Not good at all, thanks for asking though. Let me holla at bro right quick and give my niece a kiss for me."

"Will do. Hold on a second," I said, walking the phone to Wes.

He put the phone on speaker and placed it on the table next to the closet. "What up, brah?"

"Meet me at my mom's crib. I have to check on her and let her know what's going on. I've been riding around for the past couple hours and there's been no sign of that bitch Shanell. We have to figure out something," Dap said, letting out a sigh.

"I'm gon' hit Bria's line and tell her to send me Shanell's number. Do you have somebody that can run that shit? I need a muthafuckin' computer geek that can track her phone."

"I know just the person. Get that shit and come my way so we can get this shit rolling. There's some shit I want to run by you too. With everything that's been going on, I haven't had the chance. but we have the time now. I'll see you in a minute."

Dap ended the call and Wes reached into the closet and came out with a gun box. Shit, I thought I was the only muthafucka that had weapons in the house. You learn something new about a person the longer you're with them. My husband was in full street mode and I wasn't about to try and stop him from taking care of his business. In my opinion, the shit should've happened a long time ago.

"As you heard, I'm about to meet up with Dap. If you need me, call me. Don't text, call," Wes said, walking over and pulled me into his arms. "Keep your piece close to you. Shanell knows where we live and I don't want you to get caught slippin'. I don't know where she is, and I want you to be ready if she decides to show her face."

Dipping his head, he kissed me tenderly on the lips then again on my forehead. "Take Faith in the room with you tonight, just to be on the safe side."

"Be careful, Wes. I got bail money on standby. Take care of your business," I said, holding my head up to look in his eyes.

"I love you, baby. I'm so sorry for bringing all this turmoil in our lives. Trying to make up for my mistakes isn't going to solve the problem, but killing that bitch will be justice for my mama. If I go to prison, I want you to move on with your life. Don't wait for me."

"Don't worry about going away, Wes. We in this shit together. You better find Shanell before I do because we're on the same shit. I'm killing that bitch on sight. I'm going to hold you down regardless of the outcome. I made an oath and for better or for worse is what I'm sticking to. You got me for life, baby. Locked down or not, I'm ridin'."

We walked to the staircase and Wes slapped me on my butt as I made my way upstairs. I led the way to the kitchen and went out the door leading to the garage before I turned wrapping my arms around his waist. "I love you too, Mr. King. See you later."

Wes kissed me long and our tongues intertwined and my kitty cried from his touch. I had to pull away because it wasn't the time to think about sex. Wes walked to his car and blew me an air kiss.

Sadness was displayed on his face, but I knew my baby was in murder mode and shit was about to get real in the streets of Chicago.

Chapter 4

Dap

We left the morgue and my emotions were all over the place. Seeing my second mama lying on that table lifeless broke a nigga down. Never in my wildest dreams did I ever imagine seeing the day Beverly would leave this dreadful earth by the hands of another muthafucka. She may have had a straightforward attitude and told it like it was, but she didn't deserve getting killed in the vicious manner that she did.

Parting ways with Wes and my Pops, I headed straight to my mother's house because I needed to see her and let my tears flow freely. It was hard for me to hold them back after seeing Beverly, but I fought that shit to be strong for my brother and father. Shanell was wrong. She fucked up royally and had signed her death certificate with the stunt she pulled. Not only that, she took my nephew along for the ride with her and I wanted him back.

As I pulled into the driveway of my mother's house, I noticed her husband Roy's car parked outside. I couldn't stand that nigga, but if my mama liked his ass, I loved it. But I'd never sit back and act as if I liked him. That was the reason I hadn't been to my mama's house too much since I'd been back.

I got out of my car, made my way up the walkway, and climbed the stairs. After ringing the doorbell, I took a step back and looked around, paying attention to what was going on around me. The street was deserted, but a nigga like me couldn't be too laid back in these streets. The door opened and the sight of my mama brought tears to my eyes.

"Hey, my baby. I didn't expect you to be standing at my door," she said, opening her arms for a hug.

I walked into her arms and wrapped my arms around her body tightly. Tears seeped out of my eyes and my shoulders shook because this is what I was used to getting from Beverly. The vision of us stepping in her kitchen came to mind and it made me cry harder.

"What's the matter, Donovan?" my mama asked, stroking the back of my head.

Lifting my head, I wiped the tears from my face and drew her back to me. The thought of losing Beverly had me so emotional that I didn't want to let my mama go. It hurt so badly, and I didn't think it would hit me hard as it had.

"Come on in here so you can tell me what's going on," she said, trying to pry my arms away. Instead, she started backing up until we were inside the door. All the while I still had a firm grip on her. My mama led me to the kitchen table and forced me to take a seat. I gripped her left leg, placing my head against her stomach.

"Talk to me, son."

I sniffed and shook my head back and forth, trying to compose myself. The image of Beverly lying in the morgue plagued my mind and I bawled like a baby. After everything I'd done in the streets, none of that shit had anything on what I witnessed viewing Beverly's body that day.

"Ma, Beverly was murdered today. I just came from the morgue to identify her body with Pops and Wes. This shit is fucked up on all levels," I said, lowering my head.

"Oh my God! What happened, Donovan?" she asked, sitting in the chair next to me.

"We don't know exactly what happened, but we think Wes' ex did it. She got in the house some type of way and slit Beverly's throat and stabbed her at least ten times in the chest."

"What the hell! Why would she do that to that man's mama?" she asked, stunned.

"She has been doing a lot of crazy shit since Wes stopped fuckin' with her. Shanell—"

"Shanell! I told y'all something wasn't right with that bitch when y'all was younger. I don't know why Wes didn't leave her alone when she cheated on him and lost that baby! He dodged a bullet with her crazy ass."

"We actually found out today that she had the baby." My mama's eyes damn near popped out of her head. "Bria is in the hospital—"

28

"What the hell happened to Bria?" she exclaimed.

"Ma, would you please let me tell you what happened? I'm not trying to be here all night telling one story." I knew my mother was only trying to find out what went on, but she was frustrating the hell out of me every time she interrupted me while I was talking.

"Okay, go ahead. I'm listening."

"Shanell hit Bria with her car and left her for dead in an alley out west. Both of her legs are broken but other than that, she is good. Bria has been raising Wes' son as her own for the past five years. She said Shanell threatened her to keep the secret or she would kill her. The other night, she almost did just that."

My mama opened her mouth, but closed it quickly when I sent daggers in her direction with my eyes. When she didn't say anything, I continued. "Bria was upset with Beverly because she found out years ago that Beverly wasn't her biological mother."

"Oh, hell nawl! You are lying, right?" My mama was just as shocked to hear that tad bit of news as we were. "Wes Sr. was a fuckin' rollin' stone. Beverly was better than me because there was no way I would've stayed with his dog ass after having two damn kids on me! Me and Beverly had our ups and downs through the years, but after everything was said and done, it was about you having a relationship with your father. The rest of that shit was irrelevant, and I left it at that."

My mama Karla and Beverly used to go at it when I was younger. Pops was living a double life, but had a whole wife and kid at home. Every weekend I went over to their house, but it was always drama when we got there because my mama was doing the most.

"I had so much respect for Beverly because regardless of how you were conceived, she always treated you like she gave birth to you. She loved you like you were one of her own from the beginning. How is your daddy holding up?" she asked as her punk-ass husband, Roy, waltzed in the room.

"Why the fuck is you asking about that nigga?" he growled at her. I turned around and mugged his ass, but he stomped his way behind my mama. "Do you hear me talking to your muthafuckin' ass, Karla?"

"You got the game all fucked up, dude. You better lower your tone when you're talking to my mama. I don't know who the fuck you think you is, but her daddy been dead a long fuckin' time," I snapped back at him.

"Stay outta my business, D. This my house and she ain't gon' be talking about another muthafucka in my shit!"

"Correction, nigga! This *my* house! Last time I checked, I paid for this bitch with my hard-earned money. She can say and do whatever the fuck she wants to around here because I paved the way for her to do so. Let me find out you be in here puttin' yo' hands on my OG and we gon' have a muthafuckin' problem," I said, standing up and pulling up my pants.

Roy bypassed my mama and stood face to face with me. I wasn't the little boy that was scared of his ass back in the day. Dap was different than lil D, and his ass was going to find out the hard way.

"I'm still the man of this house and I'll whoop your ass like I used to do when you were younger. Don't tell me how to check my bitch!"

When the word "bitch" left his mouth, I hit his ass right in his chops. Roy stumbled back and I laid his ass out. The nigga laid on his back snoring because I put his punk ass to sleep. He had blood running from his nose and I didn't bother checking to make sure he was good. Fuck him.

"Donovan, why would you do that? He wasn't going to do nothing to me," my mama said, kneeling down beside her husband.

"You can allow him to disrespect you all day, but he won't do that shit in front of me! Every time he try it, he gon' end up on his back. When I get tired of knockin' the fuck outta him, I got a bullet with his name on it. Get mad, I don't care, you heard what I said."

The doorbell sounded and I stepped over Roy and went to open the door. It wasn't the time for anybody to come at me on bullshit because I was on one. Wes stood outside the door and I stepped aside and let him in.

"What up, brah," he said entering the crib. "What the fuck happened in here?"

"Pussy ass nigga disrespected my mama and thought I was a lame muthafucka that wasn't gon' get at his ass," I shot back at him as my mama finally got her husband up off the floor. "I'm about to leave. If I come back and there's a scratch on my mama, you better call yo' family ahead of time because they'll be pulling out their all black everything for yo' bitch ass!"

"Man, D, you didn't even have to do all that. I love your mama," Roy said, rocking back touching his nose. "I think you broke my nose."

"If you touch my mama or call her another bitch, I'm gon' break yo' ass and that's on everything I love," I said, turning to my mama. "Remember what I said. Next time, yo' husband gon' be a distant memory. I love you and I'll be back soon."

"Donovan, this is my house and you can't come in here trying to call shots. If you can't respect my home, I don't want you coming here."

I almost told my own mama to kiss my ass but instead, I just turned and walked out of the front door. Wes stayed behind for about ten minutes before he too came outside. It took everything in me not to go back in the house and kick Roy's ass again.

"Come on, Dap, that nigga ain't crazy. He's not going to do shit to Mama Karla. He knows he will die behind that shit, and I don't think he's ready for that. You did what needed to be done and she took his side. You have to let her deal with that nigga. I'll be right by your side if he gets out of pocket in any way."

"Fuck that shit! That nigga gotta go," I said, heading back toward the house.

Wes grabbed me by the arm and shook his head. "It ain't gon' happen, bro. You can put him out tonight, but he'll be right back in there soon as you leave. Don't put a wedge between you and your mama. Love her from a distance if you have to, but always be there for her. I don't have my mama no more, and I think Karla is going to be okay. Let them have this moment. I'm sure she's in there checkin' him right now."

"You right, but I'm telling you, brah, I'll kill that muthafucka!" I said heatedly. "Where's Pops?"

"He went to the hospital to break the news to Bria. He's holding it together pretty well actually. We need to find Shanell's ass."

"Oh, her time is definitely coming. She wrote a check her ass can't cash and she won't live to capitalize off the shit. Let's go to my crib. I got some other shit I want to holla at you about," I said, walking to my whip.

***

Stepping in my house, I disarmed the alarm and headed straight for the bar and grabbed the D'USSÉ bottle. Wes came inside and went straight to the kitchen and came back out with a bottle of Heineken in his hand. I made my way to the basement and flipped the switch before descending the stairs going to my lounge chair to kick back.

"What you wanted to talk about, Dap?" Wes asked, sitting on the loveseat next to me and placing his beer on a coaster.

"I got a call day before yesterday from Juice. He let me know that Rocco was killed in his crib."

"The Italian dude that helped you upgrade Customs?" Wes asked, stunned.

"Yeah. Juice said word on the street is it was a hit. I believe his own sons, Luciano and Arturro, killed him. I've been getting death threats since the day Bria came back in town. I haven't really been able to talk about it because of all the shit that has happened over the last couple days." Throwing a shot of D'USSÉ down my throat, I poured another before I continued.

"The grand opening for Customs II is next week. I can't go through with it because we have to get things together for Beverly's homegoing."

"Nah, we not pushing shit back, and don't try to go to Pops about it because he's going to say the same thing. Mama would want you to stay on schedule with your business. Nine times out of ten, her services won't be until the week after. We can have Justice and

Tana help Pops with the arrangements; it will be cool. Dedicate this shit to her, brah. Keep her spirit alive."

Wes pulled out a bag of weed and I had to do a double take because his ass was square as hell since he started working for that corporate company. We hadn't smoked together in years and deep down, I didn't think the nigga had it in him to do that shit. I watched as he broke down the weed and lined it in the wood. My bro rolled that shit like back in the day, if not better.

"Damn, nigga, you back smokin'?" I laughed at the stupid shit I asked because obviously he was.

"Man, the shit with my mama just took me back to the streets. Shanell is a dead bitch walking. She can only hide for so long, and I'll be waiting on her ass to come out. I'm still trying to wrap my head around the fact Sage is my seed." He laughed. "The bitch hid that shit real good and my own sister helped her."

"Bria was wrong for that shit and she should've said something. I don't give a fuck if Shanell threatened to do something to her. Bria let her emotions lead her in the wrong direction. If she didn't know shit else, she should've known that we would've handled that shit pronto. I'm not even going to hold her to that shit. She's going through enough. We just have to get nephew back and pray Shanell don't hurt him."

"She can act like she's crazy, but I don't think that hoe that crazy. Oh, Bria gave me the bitch's number," Wes said, taking his phone from his pocket. My phone vibrated and I looked down at it on top of the bar. "Send it to yo' people because I need to know where the fuck she's at."

"I'll get on it right now." As I picked up my phone to call Christian, a picture text came through on my phone. The number was one that I didn't recognize, but I knew it came from California and right away I was ready for some type of bullshit. Just as I expected, there was a picture of Customs and a message that said, *"This is rightfully mine, motherfucker! I'm coming for it."*

I didn't give a damn about a nigga threatening me, but I wanted him to reveal himself. What I wasn't about to do was go back and forth with this punk over the phone. The fact that he was sending a picture of my store in California meant whoever it was wasn't in Chicago.

Me: Reveal yo'self. Pick up the phone and speak yo' peace, nigga! We're not about to hide behind the phones, hit me up.

After sending Shanell's number and a quick message to Christian about what I needed, I put my phone back on the bar and turned back to Wes. He was staring at nothing in particular while blowing smoke out of his nose. The death of Beverly was hard on all of us and it was going to be hard to bounce back from. Wes picked up his phone and made a phone call.

"Hey, Nell, this is Wes, call me back. I got your number out of Bria's phone and wanted to tell you what happened to her. It's something I don't want to leave on your voicemail, so hit me back."

I was looking at his stupid ass like he was the crazy one because he shouldn't have called that hoe for shit! When he ended the call, I took another squig of my drank and just stared a hole in his ass. He passed the blunt to me and I snatched it from his hand.

"Why the fuck would you even try to call that dizzy bitch?"

"I want to see if she's gon' give me a hint on her whereabouts or where her head is at," he said.

"Shanell ain't stupid, brah. She ain't telling you shit, and I bet you all the money in your account the bitch ain't about to call your goofy ass back either. We gon' catch up with her; don't worry." My phone started vibrating and my adrenaline was out of control when I saw the number calling that had texted. The facial expression must've told Wes something was up.

"Who is that, bro?"

"Hold on," I said, connecting the call and put it on speaker. "Yeah, bitch ass nigga."

"You sure are tough over the phone, Dap. I want to see if you have that same energy when I approach you with my Ruger in your face." The person on the other end laughed.

"If you're lucky enough to get close to me with a pistol in hand, you a good muthafucka! Look, Luciano," I said, catching on to the voice with the Italian accent. "One thing I've learned is not to trust a snake muthafucka. If you could kill yo' own father over money,

34

nigga, when I see you, it's on sight! Rocco trusted me more than you and your brother. That should tell you something. It's not my fault he saw something in a thorough nigga."

"I'm coming for Customs, both of them! They belong to us!" he said, screaming into the phone. "Chicago is not going to be the same once we're finished with your ass, Dap."

"Stop selling wolf tickets and bring yo' ass, Lucci! I ain't never bowed down to no muthafuckin' body, and I'm not about to start with you. Bring that shit to my stompin' grounds. Yo' ass gon' get ate the fuck up! I put that on my mama, nigga! When you come, you better come correct and bring yo' whole army, because you gon' need them muthafuckas!" I banged on his ass and immediately got up and paced the floor.

"Dap, that nigga just threatened you in a subtle way, my nigga!" Wes said, watching my every move. "The way I'm taking this shit, he trying to ride down on ya."

I opened the walk-in closet and stepped back. "The nigga can come if he wants to. His ass gon' get carried away in a body bag. I have everything needed and more to send his ass to his maker. I'm not worried about shit Luciano is saying. Just be ready, because we gon' have to blast these niggas."

Play time was over. I already knew how Luciano and his clan was coming. It was time to bring Cali to the Chi ahead of time, because we were fighting too many demons at one damn time.

Meesha

Chapter 5

Tana

Justice called me when I was getting ready to lie down in bed for the night. I had been debating if I wanted to call Dap to come over, but decided against it because he hadn't picked up the phone to call me at all that day. When she told me that Beverly was murdered in her home, I couldn't believe it. But when she said it was Shanell's funky ass, I almost lost it!

On top of that, she took Sage and disappeared into thin air like a thief in the night. All the things that took place in a two-day period was unbelievable, and my heart went out to the King family. What they were going through was a true tragedy, and I wouldn't wish it on anyone. Even though Bria was a bitch for what she had done, I sent a prayer up for her trifling ass too. My friend was holding it together for her husband, and I was going to be there to hold her down.

"Miss Taylor, the bell rang. Is there any homework for tonight?" one of my students asked, bringing me out of my thoughts.

"I'm sorry, class. No, I'll give you all a free day tonight. Be careful and enjoy the rest of your day. Class dismissed."

The day flew by and I didn't know where the time went. I really wasn't in full teacher mode and that was not me. Nothing ever got me off my square when it came to my students, but the situation at hand sure did. When I checked my phone, I saw that I had a missed call from Donovan and decided to hit him back as I gathered my belongings.

"What's up, Sexy? I called you during your lunch break. but I guess you were busy," he said when he answered.

"The day passed me by, I'm sorry. My condolences to you and your family. Justice told me what happened. Why didn't you call me?"

"Everything happened so fast that I didn't think about calling you and that was my fault. I've been making calls trying to track Shanell down, but nothing has come through yet. I want you to watch your surroundings, the bitch is crazy and there's no telling who's on her radar next."

"I understand your concern, but Shanell isn't coming for me. Y'all need to ask Bria if Sage is capable of reaching out to her if he had to. He came off to me as a very smart kid."

"That's why I find myself growing closer to you. The things you come up with are amazing. I will have to call and ask some questions, plus I need to see how she's doing since finding out about Beverly's death." Dap became eerily quiet and I stopped in my tracks as I headed for the door of my classroom. "Tana, I have some business to take care of and I will be unreachable for a while."

From the time I started hanging out with Dap, business had never gotten in the way of us spending time together. All of a sudden, he wanted me to believe work was going to have him pushing me to the back burner? Nah, I've been around the block and back as well as running in the streets with the best of them. Something wasn't right with what he was trying to pull and I had to play this smoothly to get the truth.

"Everything that has been going on with Shanell, the bullshit with Tyson, and getting ready for Customs grand opening hasn't taken you away from me at any given time. What's so different about what's going on now that would change things up?"

"To make a long story short, there's so much going on with my family and I want to be there for them in any way I possibly can."

"Dap, don't patronize me. How about you give me the long version of what's going on because there's more to the story and you're leaving me in the dark. It would be wise for you to tell me everything because we've come too far these past couple months. If we are going to go into this relationship keeping secrets, I don't want any parts of it. That's not the way I operate."

"Tana, you're looking into this a little too much. It's nothing that will jeopardize what we have going on, I swear to you. If anything, I'm trying to protect you."

"Protect me from what?" my voice raised a couple octaves. "Tell me what's going on that I need to know about. How hard can that be?"

"The less you know the better, baby. Trust me. Call me when you get home. Okay?"

"Whatever, Dap—"

"I told you to stop calling me that shit!"

"At this point, that's what I'm going to call you because obviously you're hiding shit like a nigga doing dirt in the street. Saying you want to be there for your family is bullshit! Remember, my best friend is part of that very family so her wellbeing is my concern and I will be there through it all, just in case you forgot that tad bit of information. I will gladly text you when I arrive home."

I hung up on his ass because I knew he was hiding something from me. It didn't matter at that point. Dap didn't really owe me an explanation because we weren't exclusive. Yeah, we fucked a couple times, but that didn't warrant him having to tell me everything that was going on in his life.

I walked out of my classroom and did everything needed to end my work day. Exiting the building, I hit the key fob to unlock the doors to my car. As I backed out of the parking spot, my phone rang and I ignored it because I had nothing to say to Tyson. The ringing stopped but started ringing immediately after. It had been a while since Dap beat his ass and I guess Tyson thought it was okay to contact me again.

I turned the radio on to drown out the phone. K Michelle's *The Rain* was playing and I grooved all the way home. After I pulled into my complex, I parked, grabbing my phone. There were at least ten missed calls; all from Tyson. Shaking my head, I wondered how a man that left me was acting a plumb fool because I gave him what he wanted.

Not feeding into his harassment, I locked up my vehicle and walked toward my apartment building. A funny feeling fell over me, causing me to look around to make sure nothing was out of place. There wasn't anything out of the norm and I continued on. When I made my way to my apartment, my heart started beating fast because the door was cracked open. The door jamb had been pried open and the panel was completely ruined.

Going inside was out of the question, so I stood outside and listened for any type of movement from the inside. I peeked through the crack and my apartment was tore up! My phone rang. I looked down at it in my hand and Tyson's name was on display. Answering the phone, I was pissed because I knew his bitch ass was behind this shit.

"What, Tyson?" I barked into the phone.

"Now you want to answer the phone," he laughed. "Do you like the way I redecorated your place? You're not untouchable, Tana. Stop playing with me before I fuck you up!"

"Tyson, I see you didn't learn from that ass whoopin' my man put on you. Did breaking into my apartment and destroying everything I worked hard to provide for myself make you feel good? This is some shit a female would do! Take the loss and move the fuck on, man! Just leave me the fuck alone, damn!"

"I'll leave you alone when I feel like leaving you alone! Don't nobody leave me, Tana!"

I couldn't do anything but laugh because he couldn't be that stupid. "You left me, little stupid dude! The only thing I did was walked away from the situation, but I'm wrong? The reason behind your madness is because you know there's another man in my life and the realization of losing me has set in. I want you to know that you're barking up the wrong tree this time."

"Oh, you think shit funny? I'm gon' show you not to play with a nigga like me," he said, hanging up in my face.

Knowing that Tyson was the culprit that broke into my apartment, I went inside to survey the damage. The couches had been slashed open, my glass tables were broken, and the TV that was mounted on the wall had one of the table legs sticking out of it. Tears clouded my vision as I walked into the kitchen because all the groceries I had purchased were scattered about the floor. Flour was mixed with water and plastered on the walls, cereal and eggs were poured in the sink.

Tyson had ruined everything in my home and he wasn't going to get away with it. I walked down the hall to my bedroom, scrolling through my phone to call Dap. Soon as I pressed the call button, someone pushed me from behind, sending my phone sliding across the floor.

"I told you not to fuck with me! You gon' give me some of this pussy, bitch!" Tyson had the nerve to still be on the scene of the crime and he was trying to violate me in the worst way.

"Don't do this, Tyson!" I screamed, trying to push myself up, but it was no use.

"That nigga ain't gon' want you after I train my pussy to cum for only me. He should've killed me when he had the chance because when I catch him, he's going to die!"

He had pinned my arms over my head with one hand while pulling my skirt up with the other. The chill on my ass would've felt good under different circumstances, but I was trying to get this Negro off me. There was no way I was about to let him take my goods willingly. When I heard his zipper go down, I panicked and started bucking like a wild horse.

"Be still, bitch! You have never denied me this pussy and I'm about to get all the way in whether you want me to or not."

Tyson pried my legs open with his knees and I knew I had to do something. Throwing my body upward, I made sure to throw my head back and connected with his face.

"What the fuck!" he said, backing up a bit.

I took that opportunity to crawl away, getting to my feet.

I was snatched back by my hair and I saw stars when Tyson punched me in my left eye. My hands automatically went up in a defensive manner, but that did nothing to help block the blows he threw fiercely at my face. Falling into the wall, I could taste the metallic flavor of blood sliding down my throat from biting my tongue. The swelling in my face was instant and my eyes burned from the tears that were having trouble coming out.

Tyson grabbed me by the neck and forcefully entered my dry well and the shit felt like someone was rubbing my walls with sandpaper. My kitty was not reacting to this bullshit at all and I felt nasty and degraded. The only thing I could do was hope and pray someone would come in and intervene. Out of all the days, all of my nosy ass neighbors were deaf as fuck.

"Yeah, that nigga ain't doing this pussy no justice because this shit is still tighter than a muthafucka! Just how I like it. This will always be my shit," he grunted while pumping in and out of me.

When Tyson growled, letting me know he was about to nut in me, his grip got tighter around my neck and I couldn't breathe. My body started getting weak and my vision blurred but I couldn't do anything about what was happening to me. He pounded into me harder and I could feel my vagina tearing.

"Fuck, this shit is gooooood!" he screamed out.

After a couple more pumps, Tyson released my neck and I fell to the floor like a rag doll. Hitting my head on the hardwood floor, I was discombobulated. He had the nerve to piss on my face before he left me lying there struggling to breathe on my own. It was hard to get any air through my nose and I knew it was broken. My phone was ringing continuously, but I couldn't do nothing but listen to it until everything turned black.

***

Attempting to open my eyes, I started panicking because I couldn't complete the task. My mind flashed back to my apartment and everything that happened came rushing back rapidly. Tears flowed from my eyes and I stifled the cries that tried to escape my mouth. I was terrified because I didn't know if Tyson had taken me somewhere after what he had done.

"Help me!" I screamed out praying someone heard me.

"It's okay, baby." Donovan appeared on the side of me and I sighed in relief and let out all the hurt I was holding in. "You're safe, Tana. I got you. You're in the hospital," he said, rubbing my hair and kissing my forehead.

"Where is Tyson?" I asked, barely able to move my lips.

"I don't know, but he better be on his way to the other side of the world. When I get my hands on him, he's dead."

"My face hurts so bad, Donovan. How did I get here?"

"You called me and I heard everything. When I heard him talking shit, I tried my best to get there. I was too late and I'm sorry," he said, sitting on the edge of the bed.

"He raped me!" I howled. "I tried to fight him; I swear."

"I know you did, baby. We're not going to worry about that now. The doctor took tests and we're waiting on the results to come back. You had to be stitched up down there. He tore you a little bit. Your nose is broken. There's nothing broken in your face, but there is a lot of swelling and your eyes are bruised badly. None of that takes away from how beautiful you are though."

"You don't have to lie to me. I know I look a mess, and it's my fault because I should've never gone into my apartment. I should've called you when I noticed the door was kicked in. He peed on me," I wailed. "That nasty son of a bitch actually pissed in my face."

"Tana, I want you to rest, baby. You don't need to stress right now. Try to stay calm. I got you."

"What aren't you telling me, Donovan?" He didn't respond right away, causing all type of sirens to start going off in my head.

"Tana, you're pregnant, baby. That was the only test that came back instantly. I'm happy and pissed at the same damn time. Ya boy is a goner because he could've killed my seed."

"Pregnant? How? I mean, are you sure?"

"Yeah, I'm sure. You're in the early stages, but the doctor said you're about six weeks pregnant. They want to monitor you for a few days and make sure your nose and bruising heals good before you are discharged."

I was still stuck on the pregnant part and everything else was pretty much gibberish at that point. My hand automatically went to my stomach. The thought of me and Dap creating life together even though we weren't solely in a relationship had me worried.

"Get some rest, Tana. I'll be here when you wake up. I'm going to put a cold compression on your eyes and hopefully it will take some of the swelling away."

Feeling the coolness on my eyes took the pain away for the time being. Relaxing my head on the pillow, I thought back to the first time Dap and I had sex. I couldn't remember if we used protection or not, but it actually didn't matter because I knew he was the father of the baby I was carrying. It took me a while to drift off to sleep, but knowing Dap was by my side, I slept peacefully without worrying about Tyson coming back to cause more damage.

Chapter 6

Shanell

It'd been four days since I left Chicago after killing Beverly. Sage and I had been holed up in a hotel in Pittsburgh because I hadn't been able to get in contact with my mother. I'd waited years to confront her about how she turned her back on me when I needed her the most as a child. She chose a dead man over her own daughter. But I was back home to get all the hate I had for her out of my system.

"I'm hungry and want to go home!" Sage screamed at the top of his lungs as he stood in the doorway of the bathroom.

His little whiny ass was five seconds from getting the piss knocked out of him. All he had been doing was throwing tantrums and crying all fuckin' day. I was tired of the shit because my patience was thinning by the minute. As much as I'd told him to be a big boy and stop the crying over the years, it seemed the method wasn't working in my favor at the present time.

"If you holla at me one more damn time, Sage, I'm gon' whoop yo' ass! You ain't never going home, so sit yo' ass down somewhere!"

"I am going home, and you better stop talking to me like that! I've been trying to be a kid, but you pushing me to the limit! Take me home, Auntie Nell, I miss my mommy!" he said, stomping his little feet.

"I am your mama! How many times do I have to tell you that?"

"You ain't my mama! My mama is Bria Janae King, bitch!"

Before I knew it, I jumped up from the bed and snatched his little ass up by his arms. Dangling him in the air, I shook the hell out of him like a rag doll. "You will respect me! Please don't make me hurt you, Sage, because I will. If you open your mouth to cuss at me again, I will knock your teeth down your throat. I'm too grown to be arguing with a five-year-old. Now get over there and sit yo' ass down like I said the first time!" I said, slinging his ass onto the bed.

Sage bounced a couple times and hit the headboard. I didn't give a damn because he was out of his mind fixing his lips to call me a bitch. Sage was going to acknowledge me as his mama sooner rather than later or he was going to hate me for the rest of his young ass life. Walking to the bag I had packed, I pulled out a jogging suit and a pair of socks. I went into the bathroom and got dressed before walking back out into the room.

"I'm going to get something to eat. Don't leave this room and don't be in here acting a damn fool. I will know if you defied me, Sage, so don't try me," I said, grabbing the remote. Finding a Disney movie on the TV, I turned to him giving him a menacing glare. "Did you hear what I said?"

"Yeah, I heard you," he pouted. "I want McDonald's." Sage got under the covers and pulled them over his head. "I don't like you anymore, Auntie Nell."

"I don't give a fuck! Sage, just remember what I said and we won't have no problems." I snatched my purse from the dresser and made my way to the door. As soon as my hand touched the knob, Sage decided he had another smart remark he just had to let out of his mouth.

"My mama told you not to leave me by myself again. You hard-headed!"

"Sage, again, you're pushing me to be the bitch you called me a minute ago. I'm about to leave so I can come back, but you better not get outta that damn bed until I return. If I find out you did, you're not going to be able to sit down for a week!" I said, leaving the room and slamming the door behind me.

As I walked down the hall, I rustled through my purse looking for a piece of candy and I found a bottle of melatonin. A thought entered my mind and I had a feeling Sage was going to get my ass caught up. Thumping two of the dissolvable tablets in my hand, I turned around and went back to the room. Inserting the key, I pushed the door open and Sage jumped back in the bed when he heard me coming back in.

"What were you doing?" I asked, storming over to him.

"I—I was trying to call my mama, but the phone don't work," he cried.

"Good, because I told your lil smart ass not to get out of that bed! See, I was coming back to give you some candy but you ain't getting nothing now."

"I'm sorry, Auntie Nell. I won't try to use the phone again. I'll be quiet and look at TV, just give me the candy," he pled with his hand out.

Sage played right into my trap and I placed the tablets in his hand and sat on the side of the bed waiting for the sleep aid to take effect. Within fifteen minutes he was yawning and could barely keep his eyes open. Easing off the bed, I left without another thought. His ass wasn't getting up any time soon because I gave his ass an adult dose of that shit.

***

After doing research the night before, I finally found my lovely mother, which shouldn't have been hard for me because she still worked at the same hospital from back in the day. The only difference was, she had changed her name again because the bitch got married. But the ghost of Christmas past was about to pay her ass a visit. I'd held the venom in far too long and had to unleash the dragon.

When Greg revealed he was the one who killed my daddy, I knew there was no way she didn't have a hand in that shit. I was taking justice out on her for him and for the fuck shit she did to me all with one stone. All my adult life I went without a mother. What the fuck did I need one for now? Not a damn thang.

I was driving on the highway as the GPS led me to my destination. There was no music; only deathly silence. My mind was in a dark place and I loved every moment of it. The ringing of my phone took my eyes off the road for a split second and it was Wes calling me again. When he called a couple days ago, I purposely didn't respond to him, but I felt like fucking with his entire being that day.

"What's up, baby daddy?" I sang into the phone. "I got your message about Bria, is she okay?"

"Nah, she died, and I thought you should know. Shit has been real fucked up for our family. Sage is missing and somebody killed my mama too."

Wes' voice cracked when he talked about his dead ass mama. I didn't feel sorry for him because all he had to do was get rid of his bitch and everything would've been fine. But no, he had to shit on me and take everything I was accustomed to. The blame was all on him and he was kicking himself for decisions he'd made.

"I'm sorry to hear that, Wes. I'll try to make it over, if that's okay."

"Nah, you know that wouldn't be a good idea with my wife and all."

"Bria was my best muthafuckin' friend and Sage is my godson! I deserve to be there for him because I'm the one that gets him in the event something happens to her! Fuck yo' wife. She took over *my* family!"

I was getting pissed because Wes was still worrying about his wife over me, and that was not how it was supposed to go down. I was his shoulder to cry on for years. Now this hoe had pushed me all the way out. "I gotta go. I will hit you back later. This news just did something to me."

I hung up because for Wes to disclose all that he did, they were on to me and I knew to keep the call at a minimum just in case they were trying to trace the it. Dumb was something I had never been. I would always be three steps ahead of anyone that was coming for me. It was going to be a true cat and mouse game before they trapped me in a corner.

"Take the next exit in three miles," the GPS directed me.

From that point, my body temperature went up a notch or two and I had to let the window down. I had to control my breathing because I felt a panic attack coming on and this wasn't the time for that bullshit. I had driven too far to think about turning around without completing my mission but I didn't think I could go through with it.

"Are you stupid? Since when have you ever backed away from a kill?" the voice in my head yelled at me. "Get yo' shit together, Shanell, because if I come out, I'm never going back in. I'd advise you to do what I know you're capable of before I take over."

"Aight, I got this! Get off my ass. I know what needs to be done," I said, pulling into the hospital.

I knew my mother worked in the neonatal unit, but finding out what floor it was on was going to be a challenge because I couldn't use anyone as a scapegoat to get in. What I was about to do was risky, but I was willing to take a chance. Getting out of my rental, I went through the automatic doors and walked to the desk ahead.

"May I help you?" the woman asked.

"Yes, I'm here to see Carol Foxx. I'm her niece and I'm here to surprise her."

"What's your name? I would have to call up to let her know you are on the way."

"What part of I'm trying to surprise her didn't you understand? I haven't seen my aunt in a couple years and I'm here on business and decided to stop in. Is that alright with you?" Trying to hold my composure was beginning to be a hard task, but I knew it was a must.

"I'm just doing my job," she snapped back.

"Point me in the direction of your gift shop, please. By the time I come back, I hope you have a heart and let me up."

She lazily pointed down the hall and I went in the direction of the gift shop, but dipped off to the elevators. Reading the sign, I found the floor I needed to be on and pushed the button. When the doors opened, a nurse was getting off and I peeped her badge that should've been around her neck, hanging out of her pocket. Slightly bumping her, I swiped her badge and stuffed it in my purse.

"I'm so sorry," I apologized quickly.

"No problem," she said, rolling her eyes.

I didn't give a damn about her attitude. I had what I needed. I pushed the button for the sixth floor because that was the floor for the OR. If I didn't know anything else, that's where all the drugs were and I needed a deadly dose of something. When the doors opened, I stepped off and there was a linen closet right there. I went in search of a pair of scrubs and found some immediately.

After slipping into the clothing, I left the closet and roamed around until I found a room where an irresponsible employee had left a tray of medicated vials and needles unattended. I grabbed three different kinds and a syringe and headed back to the elevator. It was a good thing it opened immediately because there was a doctor coming down the hall in a hurry. The doors closed in his face and I pushed the button for the seventh floor.

The doors didn't open and I pushed the open button repeatedly, but stopped when I realized I needed to insert a key card. I took that moment to insert the drugs in the syringe and put it in the pocket of the scrubs. When I put the nurse badge in the slot, the doors opened with no problem. A nurse was at the desk and she nodded at me with a smile and I headed straight for the unit I knew my beloved mother was on.

When I entered, my mother was putting a baby down in an incubator and I knew that was my chance since she was alone.

"Hello, Mother," I said, closing the door and walking over to draw the blinds. She turned around fast and her eyes were big as saucers.

"Shanell, is that you?" she asked uncertainly.

"In the flesh. Why are you so surprised to see me?"

"Where have you been?" she asked, looking around the room nervously. "How did you find me?"

"I've been struggling to take care of myself since you turned your back on me. You didn't even try to check on me after Greg violated me and I ended his life. Why didn't you fight for me, Mama?"

"He didn't touch you, Shanell! I would never believe my husband did anything you claim he did! I've always wanted to reach out to you and ask why you killed him. The story you told was a bunch of bullshit and that's the reason you served time for it! The police saw right through your lies."

I laughed in her face as I inched closer to her. "You know what? You're right, I did lie about what he did to me, but he did put his hands on me. See, where your lovin' husband fucked up at was when he confessed to killing my daddy. That tad bit of information is what got his ass slit from ear to ear. He was too cocky letting that shit roll off his tongue and he had to pay for the crime he committed."

My mother made a dash for the phone on the wall. I caught up to her and slammed her to the floor and sat on her chest. "I have one question for you, and please don't lie. Did you help Greg kill my daddy?"

She turned her head and tears ran down into her ears before answering. "No, I loved your daddy. I would never hurt him because he was the one that looked out for me."

"That's hard to believe, you know. So, you're telling me it was a coincidence that you married the man that took his life and knew nothing?"

"I swear, I didn't know!" she cried, staring right into my eyes.

"That lie rolled off your tongue like butter. I see I got that lying shit honestly and it's hereditary," I laughed, reaching in my pocket. "I hope you made peace with God, because he's about to meet you at the pearly gates. I won't have that problem; I reserved my seat in hell already and I just might see you when I get there."

Without thinking about it, I jammed the syringe into the vein in her neck. Her eyes rolled in the back of her head and she started convulsing wildly. Standing to my feet, I wiped the tears from my face and dropped the syringe in the needle box before leaving the nursery the same way I had entered.

It took no time for me to get back to the rental and onto the highway. I couldn't deal with the silence, so I turned on the radio and there was an advertisement on. I was not really paying attention to it until I heard the announcer say Donovan King.

"The place to be is Customs II in Chi-town! Tomorrow night is the Grand Opening and it's gonna be litty in that joint! Customs by Dap is known worldwide and is expanding for any and every one to get their custom bling! Get your tickets now. They are still available to party with Donovan "Dap" King at Lady Loves Nightclub!"

"Dammit! I forgot all about that shit," I screamed, hitting the steering wheel hard. Glancing at the digital clock on the dash, I saw that it was almost one in the afternoon and I had to get back to the hotel. There was no time to waste. I had to get on the road back to Chicago quick fast and in a hurry. I closed the door on my past life. Now I had to either rekindle the flame I once had with Wes or put his ass out of his misery like the dog he was.

Chapter 7

Christian

It had been years since I'd been to Chicago and a lot had changed. As I walked through the lobby of the W Hotel, all eyes were on me and my entourage that walked behind me. I made the arrangements online for our rooms and I was ready to get some sleep before the ribbon cutting of Customs by Dap II. Choosing the hotel closest to the store was something I needed so I wouldn't get lost trying to get there.

"Hey, Chris, did you call Dap to let him know we were here?" Juice asked as he joined me at the counter.

"Not yet. I want to get everyone settled before I contact him," I explained giving my attention to the woman standing behind the counter. "Good morning, I have reservations under Christian Mancini."

She tapped away on the keyboard and glanced up at me for a moment before looking back at the screen. "That information is correct, ma'am. I reserved ten rooms. Are they ready?" I asked.

"Um, yes, they are. I need to see your identification and the card you used online, please."

I gave her what she requested. She compared the information and handed the cards back to me before gathering the key cards for the rooms. Placing the cards on the counter, I thanked her and started handing them out to my team, leaving my card on the counter so I didn't give it away. The suite was mine.

"Okay guys, go get settled in. This will be our home for as long as we're needed. I hope everyone left their schedules open because leaving s not an option until everything is over and done with. Meet me in my suite in four hours. We have things to discuss with Dap," I said, retrieving my card and leading the way to the elevators.

Everyone got off on the fifteenth floor as I stayed on and made my way to the top floor. Inserting the keycard in the slot, the doors opened to the room I would be living for my duration in Chicago. I walked through the luxurious living room, placing my luggage by the side of the sofa. I poured a hefty glass of scotch and sat on the stool.

Thoughts of my brother swarmed my mind and I still couldn't believe he was gone. Luciano and Arturro believed they had gotten away with what the both of them did, but the devil was a lie. I was going to act the part and let them believe everything was copasetic, then they were going to pay for taking my brother from me. Dap was going to be the one to put them in the ground, with my help of course.

I unpacked my luggage, placing clothes in the drawers and the closet. My phone rang, causing me to walk over to the bed taking a seat. Luciano's number displayed on the screen and I had to calm myself because the anger inside of me flared up.

"Ciao, Luciano," I calmly said into the phone.

"Zio Christian, stavo chiamando per controllarti, con tutto quello che é successo con papa, so che é difficile per te in questo momento." (Uncle Christian, I was calling to check on you. With everything that's happened with Dad, I know it's hard for you right now.)

I paused because this boy wanted to call like he wasn't the one who killed his dad, my brother and he wanted to send out sympathy as if it was nothing. It took everything in me not to go off on him. Taking a deep breath, I reached for my scotch and took a sip.

"I'm fine, Luciano. Haven't seen you in a while. How are you and Arturro holding up?" I asked the question, but really didn't care one way or another.

"This have been rough since Dad's passing. I was wondering, has the lawyer contacted you about his will? I haven't heard anything and I know I was the beneficiary of his estate."

That shit alone had me heated. Luciano wasn't calling to ask how I was doing; he was worried about money. It was hard trying to suppress my anger, but it had to be done. Fighting the urge to cuss him out lost its battle because I didn't have it in me to fake the funk.

"Luciano, while you're asking about money, I haven't seen you mourn the death of your father yet. What type of fool are you?"

"Look, that money belongs to me and I want it!"

"You better remember who you're talking to. Raising your voice will never shake me and I will choke a booger out of your ass. Money should be the last thing on your mind. As much as Rocco did for you and your brother, you should have money saved. Obviously, you have mismanaged your funds and don't have a pot to piss out of."

I had to let him know that I didn't appreciate the shit he came at me with. "If the house you sleep in at night wasn't paid off by Rocco, you would be homeless! Get your shit together, and you better do it fast!"

"Homeless? My father had money hand over fist and that shit goes to my brother and I. I'll never go without because I've inherited a lot with my bloodline alone. Now where the fuck is my money?"

"You have lost your fuckin' mind! How about you call the lawyer and ask him where your money is? The only cash I have is what I've earned throughout the years. That's right, I've invested and will be straight with or with Rocco. Even if he was still here, I would be alright. What about you, Luciano?"

"I have money in my account. Just not the billions that should be there. That's where you come in, Uncle Christian. You are the one that has access to the lawyer. I don't."

"Why do you think Rocco had it set up that way? I'll tell you, because you are a little ass kid trapped in a grown man's body. Your responsibility is at a fifth-grade level. To be honest, I won't be helping you contact the lawyer. You will wait for the will to be read whenever the lawyer decides to do it. Now get your spoiled ass off my phone."

"Christian, I have much respect for you and I would hate if I had to pay you a visit to get what's rightfully mine."

"Is that a threat, Lucci? If so, bring your ass on my property and you will be carried away. That's on my brother and your mother's grave. Don't fuck with me, boy. I don't know who you are scaring on the streets of Cali, but I'm not one of them punks."

"You'll be seeing me real soon, Unc. Don't say I didn't warn you."

Luciano hung up before I could say anything else. If he thought he put fear in my heart, he was sadly mistaken. He would die before I allowed him to strong arm me into doing anything on his terms.

Getting undressed, I sat on the edge of the bed, lit a Cuban cigar, and sipped my scotch slowly. Luciano and Arturro were in the very hotel I was staying in at that moment. Tapping the app on my phone, I tapped on the file I created for him and it told me what I already knew, but I wanted to keep an eye on him to make sure he wasn't on the move. Luciano threw threats and thought I was in California when I was right under his nose.

I shot Dap a text, letting him know I was in his city. Giving him the room number and time to come through, I laid back and thought about my nephews and the bullshit they were on. Luciano had to be behind everything because Arturro wasn't bright enough to put his two cents in on whatever plan they had conjured up.

***

I drifted off to sleep and when I woke up, it was almost noon. Climbing out of bed, I headed to the bathroom and took a quick shower. Throwing on a pair of black Canali slacks and a pink button-down shirt, I slipped my feet in a pair of Santoni loafers. My phone chimed, indicating I had a text. Dap was on his way up and I went to the elevator to await his arrival. When the elevator sounded, I pushed the button for the doors to open.

"What's up, Donovan? Glad you could make it, man," I said, giving him a half hug. "Drink?" I asked, walking to the bar.

"Nah, I'm good. Thanks for showing up for a nigga. I really appreciate that shit. Did you come alone?"

"Now you know I brought my whole team with me. I brought Juice and your other soldiers too, so we are packed. Everyone should be coming up any minute," I said, looking at my watch. The elevator sounded again and I smirked. "They know I love promptness."

After everyone piled off the elevator, we all sat back and flamed up whatever. I looked around the room and I was proud of the job I'd done to protect the King of Customs. I was the only one who wasn't dressed down, but I dressed like a Boss at all times and wasn't into all that street shit.

"Okay, as you all know, we are here for Donovan—" I said before I was cut off.

"Dap is fine, Unc. That Donovan shit don't fit in with what we're gearing up for." Dap laughed.

"You got it. Like I was saying, we are here for Dap because my nephews, Luciano and Arturro, are on some shiesty shit and will be coming for his head. I'm not saying he can't hold his own, because I know he can. But he is family and we will be there for whatever he needs us for," I explained.

"As you all know, his grand opening for Customs II is this evening. It has been broadcasted on many major radio stations around the country. My nephews have a few hittas on their team, but they don't have nothing on us. With my people and Dap's combined, we will come out on top in whatever they plan to do."

"They won't get the chance to pull out on my nigga!" Juice cut in with a scowl on his face. "I know that's your family and all, but they coming for the wrong one!"

"You are correct; they are my family. I'm here to let you know they won't try to pull the trigger in a crowded club. Trust me on that. We are going to go to the party and have a good time. If anything kicks off, that's when we will pounce. I doubt it will though, seriously."

"I'm not worrying about nothing, honestly. Lucci knows not to play with me. I've already told Rocco if they come for me, they are going to die," Dap said, standing to his feet. "We didn't have to meet up for this, Chris."

"You're correct. There's something else I wanted to discuss with you as well. Just to let you know, Luciano and Arturro are staying in this very hotel. They don't know we're here and I want to keep it that way. We will be ready to roll out about five o'clock so we can be in place at Customs in case they show up. The only one that'll get out is Dap's crew. The rest of us will be Dap's eyes."

"They are in this muthafucka?" Dap asked. "Call them niggas up here so we can handle this shit right now then!"

"Nope, I want them to think they have the upper hand. Trust me, Dap," I assured him. "Everyone can leave now. I need to talk to Dap about business and I'll see you all later."

Once the room was clear and Dap and I were the only ones present, I walked into the bedroom and retrieved the envelope I had brought along with me. I had put a stop to the lawyer mailing out the information Rocco left for Dap. The information was too lucrative to go through the postal service.

"I know I told you to be on the lookout for documentation from Rocco."

"It never came to me in the mail. I thought you intercepted it when I told you I didn't want it," he said, sitting back on the sofa.

"I did, but not for the reason you think. Dap, you will take this money and do with it as you choose. My brother thought highly of you and wanted you to accept his offer without any rebuttal. Dap, you deserve it. Take it, man," I said, holding the envelope out to him.

I downed the glass of scotch while he looked over the paperwork. I watched his eyes expand as he turned the pages. Dap may have been young, but he was wise beyond his years and I had faith that he would be a great investor in many things. There was no doubt in my mind that he would triple his money in less than two years.

"This is too much, Christian. I wouldn't know what to do with this kind of money, man," he stated, glancing up at me.

"Sign your name on the dotted line and find out. The minute I fax the documents back to Sylvester Todd, you will have access to your new business account. All the cards and checks will come to you in the mail tomorrow. The deed to Rocco's house is already in your name, as well as the cars. Oh, you get to keep the lawyer and his financial advisors too. You're set for life, and I will be there with you every step of the way."

Dap sat scratching his head. "Have you seen Rocco's house? That muthafucka is huge! It's too much house for me, Christian."

"Stop making excuses and sign that shit! Sell that muthafucka if that's what you want to do, it's yours," I laughed.

"Give me a pen. I will sign these papers, but I won't make any decisions on the assets just yet. There's so much going on with my family right now. My stepmom was murdered last week by the woman whose phone number I gave to you. As a matter of fact, have you been able to track that hoe?"

"Sorry for your loss. I'm here if you need me," I said sincerely. "There haven't been any movements on her phone," I said, pulling the app up on my phone. Showing him the file that I named crazy bitch to prove it was dead. "I got a ping on it the other day, but she wasn't on it long enough to pick up the signal. She has to be a smart one that she cut her calls very short."

"She's going to slip up soon," Dap said, rising to his feet. "Do what you have to do with those papers. I have to go home to get dressed, then head to the hospital to see my sister before the grand opening. Thanks again, man. I appreciate you."

"No problem. There's nowhere but up from here. Once we close these doors of negativity, you can start your new life. It feels good when you're at the top, Dap. I have one request. Keep your wealth to yourself. It's true about what they say, mo' money, mo' problems."

"I already know. Hell, these muthafuckas think I'm ballin' off Customs. I am, but not like this," he laughed. "Let me get out of here. You gave me a lot to think about," he said, pushing the button on the elevator.

When the elevator doors opened, I gave him a fist pound and let him go about his day. I had plans to work on business until it was time for me and the crew to leave the hotel.

Meesha

Chapter 8

Bria

I was still lying in the hospital and there was nothing I could do about it. Shanell was one evil bitch, and helping her deceive my brother was something I regretted. Leaving her alone was what I should have done years before shit got out of control. When my daddy told me Beverly was murdered, I cried so much I made myself sick and had to be injected with medication to calm me down.

Sage was constantly on my mind and I hoped every minute he was alright. I never thought Shanell would do the things she had done, but I should've known not to trust her as much as I had. She was toxic and I'd lost the only mother I've known because of her. Not getting the chance to actually mend our relationship had part of me feeling like I died along with her. If it wasn't for my baby, I would find a way to end it all and make the pain go away faster.

The door opened and my brother walked in looking sharp as fuck in his get up. Dap had on a pair of Givenchy jeans with a black Givenchy shirt to match. As I scaled his body down to his feet, I saw that he had on a pair of black and maroon Givenchy sneakers that had to have cost him a grip. My brother was doing the damn thing with his business, but I didn't know he was doing it like that.

"What's up, big head?" he asked, taking a seat in the chair next to my hospital bed.

"Nothing much. Where you on your way to looking all spiffy and shit." I chuckled.

"The grand opening for Customs II is tonight. I wanted to stop by to shoot the breeze with you for a minute and see how you were doing. Pops will be here soon to sit with you. Even though Shanell thinks you're dead, we don't want to take no chances."

I picked at the blanket that covered my body without looking in his direction.

"Talk to me, Bria. What's on your mind?"

Guilt was eating me up from the inside and knowing I let everybody down in my family was a hard pill to swallow. Life was short, and I had to make everything right with the people that continued to stand by my side after the shit I'd put them through. I just didn't know where to start with Dap.

"Donovan, I'm so sorry." The tears flowed freely and I couldn't stop them from falling down my face. "You have every right to be upset with me and I will truly understand if you never come see me again."

"Bria, I'm not upset with you. Disappointed, yeah. What's done is done, sis. You came clean about what you were holding in for years. I'm pissed because you didn't come to one of us about what you had gotten yourself into. Keeping Sage away from us, especially Wes, was fucked up. He can never get those years back with his son. Now he has to worry if that bitch Shanell has harmed him in any way."

"I'm sorry! I've wanted nothing but the best for that little boy. He's not just my nephew. Sage is my son! I raised him when I was barely an adult myself and I gave him the best life any kid could ask for. If anything happens to him, I would die, Dap. Please find him."

"Come on, stop that shit. You may as well let it all out while you can. Don't hold nothing back."

"Beverly—Beverly is dead and it's my fault," I wailed. "Since I found out she wasn't my mama, I didn't view her as the mother she had been. I felt betrayed and never wanted to come home because I didn't want to face her. Pretending to be something I knew I wasn't didn't sit well with me. But when I had the opportunity to squash everything, I didn't. The animosity was still in my heart."

"Her death is not your fault. Answer this question for me, though. How is it that you didn't have the same anger towards Pops that you had for Beverly?" Dap asked, folding his arms over his chest.

"I don't know why I wasn't upset with him. You know I've always been a daddy's girl and he could do no wrong. I always blamed Beverly because in the back of my mind, I always felt it was her idea to keep the truth from me. Even when Daddy told me otherwise, I wasn't trying to hear what he was saying. I was wrong for placing all the blame on her. She didn't deserve that."

62

Paid in Karma 3

"Stop crying. We will get through this together. Beating yourself up is not going to change what has already happened. We can't reverse the past, but we can make the best out of the future. We may have been at odds because of the things you have done, but we can build something new. We will always be family; nothing will ever change that."

Dap rose to his feet and leaned down, planting a kiss on my cheek. Hugging his neck tightly, I cried trying to cleanse my soul but it wasn't helping. I finally released my brother and pain shot up my legs and I howled out.

"Are you alright?" Dap asked with sincere concern.

"Get the nurse. I need something for the pain in my legs." It took a lot out of me to say those few words.

Donovan pushed the call button and a nurse came into the room immediately. "What can I help you with, Bria?"

"I'm hurting. Can you please give me something for this pain?" The tears were flooding down my face and I couldn't even lift my arm to wipe them away.

Nurse Kim knew the pain was real because she left and came right back. She injected a small amount of morphine into my IV, and the pain started to subside. She stood over me and I closed my eyes.

"I'm doing a double today so I'll be here with you all night. I'll be back to check on you in a bit. Get some rest. The medication is about to force you to do so even if that wasn't in your plans," she laughed. "You'll be alright, Bria."

"Sis, I'm about to head out. I'll be back tomorrow to tell how things went with the grand opening. Oh, I thought you would like to read these while you're here," I said, pulling the stack of letters from my back pocket.

"Okay, bro, and thanks for not giving up on me." I smiled. "I think these letters will give me a little bit of peace."

"That will never happen and I hope so. Pops should be here soon, but in the meantime, sleep, Bria."

Meesha

Chapter 9

Justice

I wasn't in the party mood, but I had to go represent Dap in Tana's absence. It was like everything bad was happening back to back and I had a funny feeling about this grand opening. In all honesty, I wished Dap would've postponed his event for another day but after getting the go ahead from his father, he pushed forward. Tana even wanted the show to go on after what happened to her.

Tyson was a whole bitch for the shit he did, but he had signed his death certificate. Both Wes and Dap added his ass to the kill list right along with Shanell, but they better hope they found her first. She could've left Wes' mama out of her tirade and focused on his ass. Wes was going through it, especially after finding out Sage was his son.

We had a long discussion about it and I was standing by him. Whenever we got Sage back, I was ready to welcome him into our family with open arms. It wasn't like he cheated and made a baby. He was cheated out of knowing Sage even existed, and that was fucked up.

"Damn, wifey!" Wes whistled as he entered the bathroom, wrapping his arms around my waist. "You're wearing the hell out of this dress! No one would believe you had a baby three months ago," he said, grabbing a handful of my ass.

I was putting the finishing touches on the nude makeup I decided to wear for the night. The black sequin dress I had on had a deep plunge in the front that showcased my breasts, which still sat high without a bra. The bottom cut at an angle with black feathers and showed off my thighs perfectly. I had on a pair of crystal Louboutin heels that sparkled when the light hit them with a fresh French manicure on my toes.

"Ass fat, yeah, I know," I rapped as I grinded into him.

"Don't start nothing you can't finish. You look beautiful, baby," he said, kissing my cheek.

"Thanks. I'm almost finished. We have to get out of here because Tana is anxiously waiting on us to bring Faith over."

"Dap don't live too far, so we have plenty of time. I got these for you," he said, handing me a jewelry box.

Placing the makeup brush on the counter, I turned and took the gift from his hand. As I lifted the lid slowly, the chandelier diamond earrings were glistening in the light. They were beautiful! Quickly taking one of the earrings out of the box, I placed it in my ear and beamed from ear to ear.

"Bro had these custom made just for you. It's the only pair out there, so none of these females can say they had them first."

"Well, these are beautiful, and I'm going to tell Dap to sell these to anyone that wants them. He will definitely get that cheddar, no doubt," I said, putting the other earring on.

I picked up the makeup brush and ran it across my nose before stepping back to observe myself in the mirror. Wes was matching my fly with his black Armani suit and silver accessories. I stepped out of Wes' arms and walked back into the bedroom, going straight to the closet.

"You're dressed, Justice. What else do you need?" Wes said, appearing in the doorway. I attached the holster to my upper left thigh and adjusted it so it would be well hidden. "No, you don't need that! You're going to be with me."

"I may not need it, but I'd rather be ready just in case," I said, placing my nine inside the holster. Adjusting my dress, I turned to the floor length mirror and moved from side to side to see if my weapon of choice was visible to the eye. It wasn't. "Okay, I'm ready. Go get Faith while I grab my clutch and phone. I'll meet you downstairs. Her bag is already packed on the dresser."

I hit Tana with a text letting her know we were on our way. She had been staying with Dap since Tyson broke in her apartment and I was glad she didn't put up a fight about it. Dap didn't give her much choice in the matter anyway. He and Wes cleaned out her place and only brought her clothes and personal items back. All the rest of that shit was thrown away.

As I walked down the hall towards Faith's room, Wes was coming out with her in his arm. He held out the baby bag and nodded his head for me to head for the stairs. I stood by the front door as I watched my husband step off the last step looking sexy as fuck in a black Armani button down shirt and a pair of black slacks. The black Balenciaga shoes he wore showcased his size thirteen feet and he definitely had the dick to match.

When he walked out of the house and down the stairs, I locked up the house after setting the alarm and followed him to his brand-new black Range Rover. Wes had left one day and returned with the truck and I wasn't even mad because it was nice and he needed to smile for a change. It was something he rarely did since Beverly was killed. If it wasn't for Dap's grand opening, he would be right at home with Faith and me.

Wes placed Faith in her car seat and made sure she was secured and closed the door before side stepping to open the door for me. Once I was seated and buckled in, he closed the door and made his way around to the driver's side of the truck.

"You are so beautiful, baby," he said as he leaned over and kissed my cheek as he started his new toy.

"Thank you." I blushed like a school girl because the smile displayed on his face was making my lower region tingle. The aroma of his Clive Christian cologne had me damn near wagging my tongue like a puppy. Being enclosed in the truck made it fill my nostrils. I got a good whiff of his scent and I really liked it.

"I'm gon' have fun getting you out that dress." He smirked as he backed out of the driveway.

"Shid, we can find a secluded area if you want to. My candy land misses you just as much as you miss her."

"Is that right? We'll see, Miss Frisky," he laughed.

It took no time for us to get to Dap's because he only lived fifteen minutes from us. Wes pulled into the driveway, threw the car in park, and got out. I reached for the handle and he shot me a dirty look. I chuckled, but didn't open that damn door. Wes opened the door and went to get Faith out of the back. I walked up the driveway toward the house and the door opened.

"Hey, bestie! You lookin' good as fuck in that dress!" Tana said, stepping out on the porch.

"Get in that house, girl! It's cold as hell out here," I said, climbing up the stairs.

"I'm cool. This is the most air I've gotten since I was released from the hospital. Give me a hug. You are so cuuuute!" she squealed. I walked into her outstretched arms and hugged her long enough to get her ass to go back into the house. "Bring my Niecy Pooh, Wes," she said, releasing me as he walked up the stairs.

"You need to keep yo' ass in the house!" Wes' snapped at Tana. "You out of yo' mind and you don't even have on any shoes."

"Man, hush all that shit up. I needed some fresh air and I saw y'all pull up and decided to greet y'all from here. I'm good. Did you take my surprise to Customs like I asked, brah?" Tana asked, leading the way into the house.

"Yeah, that portrait was dope. You have a talent that can't be touched and you chose teaching?"

"It's my passion. I love the kids and it goes beyond teaching. Many of my kids need a nurturing place to express themselves and feel part of something. I'm the teacher who gives them that and more. Every single day I feel the love my students bestow on me because I give it to them ten times fold."

"That's what's up," Wes replied as he took Faith out of her little coat. "The kids of today need that guidance because some of their parents don't give a fuck about them. If more teachers had your thought process, more of these kids would have a positive attitude. Then again, that shit starts at home. Do you feel what you do is a waste of time? I ask because you may give positivity, but they go right to the negativity when they are away from you."

"That's true, and no, I don't feel it's a waste. It actually allows me to push that much harder to see the positivity in the words I speak about. It takes a village, Wes, and I'm right in the middle fighting to prevent my students from being statistics. They already have one strike against them, and that's being born black."

"I feel you, and keep doing whatever you have to do to keep their heads in the books and off the streets. You have eighth graders,

Tana. High school is rougher, and it's the place where they will need the most guidance."

"Wes, yeah, I know, and that's what I'm afraid of. Hopefully what I'm trying to instill in them follows a good percentage of them through the next four years." Tana sighed. "Anyway, you loved the portrait, huh?"

"Hell yeah, I did! You captured it beautifully and Dap is going to love it too," he said, walking over with a sleeping Faith.

"I'll be right back. Put her milk in the fridge, Justice," Tana said, disappearing up the stairs.

"Hurry, we have to get out of here," I said, removing my fur before taking Faith's milk to the kitchen.

As I exited the kitchen, Tana was making her way back down the stairs with a big ass wrapped package in her hands. She walked up to Wes and I took Faith from his arms, stepping back slightly. Both Wes and I were confused as to what she had for him, but I didn't say anything. I just stood back and watched everything unfold.

"Wes, I wanted to present something to you as well to hold dear to your heart. So, while I've been holed up like a prisoner to heal, I did what I loved to do and made something for you," Tana said holding out the package. "I hope you like it."

Wes slowly tore the paper from the package, revealing a black frame. Once the paper was removed completely, he held the picture up and tears fell from his eyes. "This is beautiful, Tana! Your talent is phenomenal, and I will cherish this for all the years to come. It's like my mama is right here with me. Thank you."

He grabbed my best friend by her arm and pulled her into his chest as he wept silently. When he released her, I stepped forward because I wanted to see what had my husband so emotional. Drying his eyes, Wes looked down at the picture again and shook his head with a small smile on his face.

"Turn it around, baby so I can see," I said, feeling left out.

Finally letting me in on his gift, he did as I asked and my breath caught in my throat because the portrait of Beverly and Wes appeared to be in 3D and popped from the canvas. Wes and Beverly both wore all white as they stood in front of the bluest waters I'd ever seen. The picture was taken on our honeymoon to Jamaica. Wes wanted to make the moment a vacation for his parents as well.

"Wow, bestie, that is very pretty and you captured the moment precisely. Damn, that woman is going to be missed by all of us," I said sadly, hugging my daughter tight.

"I'm sorry for making you shed a few tears, Wes. Dry that shit up and go have a good time. Give me my niece and get out of here."

Handing Faith to Tana, I kissed her on the forehead and picked my fur up from the back of the couch. Wes was still looking at the picture until I placed my hand on his arm. He looked down and lowered his head kissing me softly on my lips.

"Thanks again, Tana. Take care of my baby. If anything seems suspicious, Dap has pistols in the basement in the back closet. There's also a gun in the drawer of the coffee table, and on the shelf in the coat closet. He also has a couple in the bedroom. Use them muthafuckas if you have to."

"Yeah, he read down all of that to me before he left. Get out before y'all are late. Justice, keep them bitches off my nigga." Tana laughed at her last statement, but she was dead serious.

"Dap is a grown-ass man. I'm not about to be babysitting nobody. That's why your ass got Faith." Opening the front door, I walked out and Wes followed. Tana waited until I was damn near to the truck before she called out to me.

"Don't forget to keep them hoes off my shit!" she yelled, slamming the door.

I couldn't do nothing but laugh as Wes opened the door for me and I climbed inside after putting the portrait in the back.

"Let me find out she's undercover crazy," Wes laughed.

It was good to hear him laugh out loud. I just had to get him through the funeral and hopefully putting Shanell in the ground so Beverly could meet her halfway to kick her ass before she walked through the pearly gates to live it up.

Chapter 10

Dap

Bria was sleeping like a baby when I left her at the hospital. I was skeptical about leaving her there alone and wanted to wait until my father arrived, but there wouldn't be a grand opening without me being there. As I walked out of the automatic doors, I saw someone that looked like my uncle Spencer walking across the lot. Staring the guy down, I waited until he got closer and off back, I knew it was him.

"What up, Spence?" I called out, walking toward him.

"Damn, nephew! You out here shittin' on these young niggas." We slapped hands and he bumped chests with me. "Yo' ass done grew up on me," he said stepping back.

Spencer was my Pops' older brother and he was my favorite uncle growing up. I didn't even go see him when I got back in town. Shit, so much had happened in the months since I'd been back and it hadn't even crossed my mind.

"I'm a King's man now." I smirked. "You going to see Bria?"

"Yeah, but I'm going stay up here with her while y'all at the grand opening. Yo' daddy wanted to be there for you. Congratulations by the way, nephew. I'm proud of you. I was thinking back to when you started Customs and it was just t-shirts then. Now, you going all out making some real dough. I'm glad you stuck with it, man."

"There was no other way. You and Pops instilled hard work into us at an early age. Quitting was never an option. I knew where I wanted to take Customs from day one. Where it is today, I never saw it getting to the level it has."

"Hard work pays off, but I won't hold you. Get to your event and we will catch up tomorrow. I have to help Wes Sr. with Bev's homegoing. We both decided to do things ourselves. This shit is unbelievable," Spence said looking up to the sky. "We have so much to discuss so I'll hit you and Wes up when I get to the house tomorrow. Be careful out there, nephew and enjoy your success."

"Okay, Unc. It was good to see you and I won't take so long seeing you."

"It's all good. Have fun tonight," he said walking into the hospital.

Hopping into my ride, I made a dash to the expressway, trying to get to Customs soon as possible. I had met up with the planner earlier to do a walkthrough of the store and the club to make sure everything was on point. Satisfaction was the only thing I could come up with when I saw both places. Autumn had done a fantastic job and earned a hefty tip for her hard work.

There were plenty of cars lined up on Michigan Avenue. The police had the street blocked off for the event and I was glad because there was nowhere for all of these muthafuckas to park. The media was there, and that was only because the mayor was going to be in attendance.

When I stepped out of my whip, everyone started clapping and the first person I saw was my father. Wes and Justice were standing next to him as well as my niggas from Cali. Juice was the first person to greet me and I hugged that nigga like it had been years since I had seen him. Kato, Fife, Judge, and Tools followed suit and a nigga felt like he was back on the West Coast. I knew Christian was somewhere watching my every move.

The renovations went better than I thought and I ended up buying the whole building because I decided to set up shop in one spot. Customs was now three stories and it was bomb. I couldn't wait for all the invitees to see how a real nigga from the Chi rolled up and made shit happen. The mayor held his hand out for me to shake his hand and I did so with much grace. I was a hood nigga but there was a time and place for that and at the moment, I was on my business shit.

"Congratulations, Mr. King. You chose a mighty fine spot to set up your establishment. It will add lots to Chicago once the tourists hear about this place."

"Thanks for coming and getting the word out on Customs. This is going to be big," I said, smiling from ear to ear.

"Well, let's get this show on the road," he said, stepping up to the microphone that was set up outside of my store.

"Good evening. I'm standing outside of the new establishment of Donovan King. Mr. King was born and raised here in Chicago and after graduating from Simeon High School, he moved to California to open a T-shirt shop that he calls Customs by Dap. Mr. King started this business as a teenager and has grown it into something spectacular. Not only has Mr. King started selling apparel, he has ventured off into custom jewelry as well."

The patrons applauded loudly, causing the mayor to pause for a few seconds.

"Mr. King recently branched into selling high-end music equipment for all DJ's and music producers to get any and everything they would need to produce what Mr. King calls "dope music". I'm all for this addition to the Magnificent Mile, and I think it would be a great asset for the city of Chicago. Thank you, Mr. King, for choosing Chicago as home for Customs by Dap II."

The drape that was hiding the sign for Customs II was revealed. It was official, and my business was about to be in full effect.

Stepping to the mic, I cleared my throat before speaking. I closed my eyes and I saw Beverly's face behind my eyelids and almost broke down on national television, but I composed myself quickly.

"Thanks to everyone that took the time to come out in support of me and Customs. This moment is something I've been looking forward to for a minute. It's a bittersweet moment because I have my family here with me except for one special person." Taking a deep breath, I looked over at my pops and he patted his chest. I nodded and continued.

"I'm going to dedicate Customs II to my second mother, Beverly King, who was tragically murdered last week. This one is for you, Sweet Lady. I did it, and I know you are smiling down on me. I will make you proud," I said, leaving the podium.

More could've been said, but after thinking about Beverly, I was ready to show off Customs so I could get to the club. The shit was selfish, but that's where my head was at the time.

The mayor held out a pair of scissors and I handed them to my father. He was the one I wanted to officially open my place of business. When he cut the blue ribbon, the cheers were loud and I stood with my chest poked out.

"Welcome to Customs by Dap II in Chicago!" I yelled, opening the door to allow everyone to enter.

The first thing I saw was a huge portrait of me and Beverly sitting and having a deep conversation at her home. The image had so much detail that I couldn't even thug it out and not cry. I missed her so much and the muthafucka that took her away from us would pay in blood.

***

An hour later, I was locking up Customs II with my family by my side. My mama showed up, and I was glad she left Roy's bitch ass at home.

"Donovan, where did you have the picture of Beverly done? It is beautiful."

"I don't know where it came from, to be honest," I said, hugging her close.

"Tana drew that for you." Wes smiled. "I brought it down earlier while Autumn was here and put it on the wall so it would be the first thing people saw when they walked in."

"Damn, I'm gon' have to say thanks in a special way when I get back to the crib. Tana is winning all kinds of points with the way she's holding shit down with me. I couldn't have done any of this without her."

"When am I going to meet this mystery woman?" my mother asked, looking up at me.

"Oh, she's no mystery. I haven't had the chance to bring her through because of everything that's been going on. Soon as she's healed, I'll bring her to the house to formally meet you. I have a surprise to tell you, but I'll reveal it when I bring her over."

"Okay, I'm going to hold you to that. You have fun at your party. I'm going to head home. These old bones can't compete with you young folks in no club." She laughed kissing my chin.

"I love you, Ma. Drive safe."

"I love you too, baby," she said, waving at everyone. "It was good seeing y'all."

"Son, I'm going to walk your mama to her car and then I'm heading to the hospital with Bria."

We said our goodbyes to Pops as he walked to catch up with my mama and I turned to my people.

"Let's hit Lady Loves and pop these bottles!" I said, throwing my hands in the air. "Plus, it's colder than a muthafucka out here. I miss the sunshine and warmth of Cali. This shits for the birds. How do y'all do it?" I asked, damn near running to my whip. Starting up my BMW, I grabbed my phone and called Tana on Facetime while I waited for my shit to warm up.

"Heyyy, handsome," she sang in the phone when she answered.

"What are you up to?"

"Me and Faith is chillin'. How was the opening? I saw your fine ass on TV."

"You liked what you saw, huh?" I smirked at her.

"Hell yeah! Did you like my surprise?"

"About that. When did you have the time to do it without my knowledge?"

"I have my ways. Did you like it?"

"Like it? I loved it! Thank you so much, baby. I'm gon' have someone come in and add 'RIParadise Beverly King' on the wall."

"Why pay someone when you have your own personal artist at your fingertips? Soon as I'm better, I'll get right on it."

I pulled out behind Wes as he led the way to the club. Placing the phone in the holder on the dash, I glanced down at Tana briefly as I drove down the street. Her natural hair was all over her head, but it didn't take away from how beautiful she was. She had on a white *"Meesha's Pen Spit Fire"* shirt that she had me to purchase from an author named Meesha Turner on social media. Tana showed me some of her posts and that woman is crazy as fuck and has me rollin' on a daily.

"Well, have fun tonight. Sorry I couldn't be there to celebrate with you, but I got you when you come home," Tana said, licking her lips. The gesture alone had a nigga brickin' up.

"You better have my pussy ready for me too. I don't want to hear that I'm asleep shit either."

"If I'm asleep, I'm here to tell you to get in where you fit in. I'll be ass out and ready. Get off my phone," she laughed. "Enjoy yourself, baby, and toss a shot back for me."

"Sure will. I'll see you later, Tana," I said as I pulled into the valet line.

There were cars all over the place and the line was wrapped around the corner. Muthafuckas wasn't playing. They wanted to party with the kid and I was all for it. I stepped out of my whip looking like Mike Lawry in *Bad Boys*. The bitches were trying to get close to a nigga like bees to honey, but my Cali clan wasn't having that shit. They were strong arming the shit out of them as we made our way into the club.

Jay Z's *The Ruler's Back* blared through the speakers as we were escorted to the VIP section. We were deep in that bitch and the club was almost filled to capacity. The DJ spotted the entourage and shouted us out.

"Ay, the Kings are in the building! Congratulations on the opening of Customs by Dap II! Let the party begin! What up, Dapski!"

Throwing my hand in the air, I continued up the stairs and sat on the sofa as a stream of barmaids made their way up with bottles of liquor. Juice came strutting his ass into the section with a slew of bitches behind him. I was with the shit because we were about to turn up in that muthafucka.

"Dap! We in this bitch! Cali in the muthafuckin' house! Time to show 'em how we do this shit on the west coast!"

I held up a bottle of D'USSÉ to salute my nigga. Having his ass with me was what I needed at the moment to keep my mind off celebrating while one of my main ladies was laid up in a mutha-fuckin' freezer in the morgue. Pouring a double shot, I tossed it back and refilled it and downed that too.

"You good, bro?" Wes asked, sitting on my right while Justice took a seat to my left.

"Yeah, I was just thinking about Bev. I'm cool though."

"Bro, we can't change what has taken place. Tonight's about you and your accomplishments. She would want you to celebrate it up. We're not about to be on that sad shit because we have to endure the shit next week. Poppin' bottles and making the clouds thick is what we on right now."

Wes produced a big-ass bag of green, wasting no time breaking that shit down and rollin' up. I threw a pack of Russian Cream woods at him to let him know we were on the same page. Justice gave me a hug and squeezed me tight to let me know she was right there with me as well. The music changed and Missy's *For My People* flowed through the club and she got up and fucked the floor up.

I didn't think she had it in her because she was so laid back, but sis was getting that shit and I was impressed. Some of the hoes in our section had the look of envy on their faces, but Justice didn't pay their asses no type of attention. Wes handed me the blunt he had rolled for me and I blazed that muthafucka up and erased all sad memories from my mental. Wes sat back puffing on his blunt while admiring his wife from afar.

A nigga had the nerve to make his way up the stairs and posi-tioned himself behind her, making the mistake of grabbing Justice around the waist. I knew from back in the day that shit wasn't going to sit well with my brother. Justice turned around swiftly and pushed the dude off her and words were exchanged.

Wes stood to his feet, pulling his pants up before storming to his wife's aid. The nigga had a scowl on his face as he pointed his finger in Justice's direction. Without warning, Wes knocked that nigga's head between the railings of the stairs and stomped his ass. Juice and the rest of my niggas jumped to their feet as a couple of dude's homies ran up the stairs to save his ass.

I jumped up when one of the niggas swung on Wes, and it was lights out for him. Rockin' his ass in the mouth, blood flew out along with a couple of his teeth. He hit the floor like a rag doll and I picked him up by the front of his shirt, only to make his ass kiss it again when I fed him a two-piece combo. Security rushed up deep and broke up the mayhem.

"What the fuck, Dap!" one of the guards yelled over the music.

"Save that shit and get these muthafuckas outta here," I said, walking back to the sofa and picking up my blunt. Justice came over and sat down beside me and Wes sat in his original spot.

"I'm sorry, y'all—"

"You don't have to apologize for that nigga's fuck up!" Wes said across the table. "I read yo' lips and you told the muthafucka to get away from you. He didn't comprehend what the hell you said and kept pressing, which led to his ass having to go to the emergency room. How many times did you have to tell his ass no?"

"Sis, that shit was foul, and that nigga was on some disrespectful shit. It was ya man's job to chin check that nigga just like he did. It's over and done with now. He and his homeboys will think twice about how they approach the next female in that way. The hands and feet that were placed on their ass tonight will be embedded in their memories from this day forward."

I saw movement out of my peripheral as I was talking to Justice and turned my head slowly. Instantly getting heated, I sat back and puffed on the blunt in my hand. My eyes locked on the woman that stepped into our section wearing a pair of black high-waisted slacks with a green bustier that had her breasts sitting up high and a pair of green Giuseppe Zanetti open toed stilettos on her feet.

It'd been almost a year since I'd seen this bitch and she had the nerve to show up to my event like everything was cool. When I was working my ass off to get my business off the ground, she pretended to be there for me, then went ghost on my ass for whatever reason. I didn't want to hear shit that came from her mouth now that I was on my feet.

"Hello, Donovan."

"Kalene, what are you doing here?" I asked, never moving an inch in her direction.

She looked down at Justice and turned her nose up. Her mind was on the wrong shit because Justice wasn't even paying attention to her ass. I let the thoughts that I knew were dancing in her mind steer her wrong. My arm was draped across the back of the sofa and for someone that didn't know the truth, it would appear as if Justice and I were an item.

"I figured I'd come and congratulate you in person on your accomplishments."

I laughed at her, sitting up as I reached for the D'USSÉ bottle. "You still drinking that shit?"

"What the fuck do you want, Kalene?" I snapped at her, slamming the bottle down on the table. "You disappeared out of my life and you should've stayed gone. I don't know why the fuck you're standing in my face right now because I don't have shit for you. Go back where you came from."

"Would you come outside so we can talk?"

"Say whatever you want to say right here. You had plenty of time to pick up the phone to speak yo' piece and you didn't. My number hasn't changed."

"Would you give us a minute?" she asked Justice nastily.

"She ain't giving you shit, Kalene!" I said, leaning my elbows on my knees.

Kalene thought she was going to waltz her prissy ass in this club looking like she stepped off the cover of a magazine and I would fall at her feet. I'll leave that up to them punk-ass Hollywood niggas because she got the wrong one thinking Donovan King was gullible. That shit didn't work on me.

"You're going to let your bitch stop you from having a conversation with me?"

"That's strike one. Watch your tongue, Ebony Barbie, you're not in California, baby. In case you forgot, you're in Chicago and will get dragged around this club," Justice said calmly. "You better direct your shit towards Dap and Dap only." Justice got up and walked over to Wes and kissed him on the lips. "Baby, I'm going to the restroom. I'll be right back."

"I'll go with you," he said, getting ready to stand to his feet.

"No, I'll be alright. I won't be gone long."

Justice rolled her eyes at Kalene as she walked past to go downstairs. Kalene sat down next to me and placed her hand on my thigh. I politely removed it and scooted away from her. She smacked her lips and looked around the table with her nose turned up.

"Would you order a bottle of Dom Perignon?" Kalene had the nerve to ask.

"No. I'm going to ask you for the last time, what the fuck is you doing here, Kalene?"

"I miss you, Donovan. There are reasons why I left California. If you give me a chance, I'll explain everything to you. How about we have a good time and then we can discuss it at your place?"

"That shit ain't gon' happen. Look, Kalene, I have a woman at my crib, so there's no room for you in my life. I'm not the type of nigga that lets a bitch walk out without probable cause and allows her back in my life. I don't have time for whatever games you're trying to play. There's nothing for us to talk about. You don't have to leave this club, but you have to get the fuck out of my section."

"But—"

"Get yo' ass the fuck away from me, Kalene!" I said, grabbing her by the back of her neck.

I wasn't the type of nigga to put my hands on a female, but I was getting tired of the bullshit Kalene was trying to pull. She got up and stared at me for a few seconds before she turned and walked away.

A few minutes later, Justice rushed up the stairs and pushed her way through the people that were looking down at the main dance floor.

"I think I just saw Shanell sitting at the bar," she said when she made it to us.

Chapter 11

Shanell

I drove the whole eleven hours back to Chicago after I left Philadelphia, only stopping to get food and to let Sage use the bathroom. His ass was really getting on my nerves and he almost died fifty-eleven times fucking with me. All he did was whine about wanting to go home to Bria. His little heart was going to be hurt once he found out the bitch was deader than a doorknob.

About five hours into the ride, I gave his ass some more of the strawberry candies I gave him at the hotel back in Philadelphia. Knocked his ass out so I could drive in peace the rest of the ride home. When I crossed the state line, I carried him inside the hotel to get a room for a few days. Making sure I stayed clear away from the city, I got a room in Schaumburg. Sage and I went out to eat once we were settled and I took a nap before getting ready to hit the club.

Sage woke me up with that crying shit again and I had to whoop his little ass. I gave him one of those old-fashioned whippings that put his ass right to sleep. After that, I got in the shower. I washed quickly and got out. With a towel wrapped around my body, I dug around in my bag and removed a red bodycon dress and a pair of black stilettos to wear to club Lady Love.

It didn't take long for me to get dressed, but I knew Sage was bound to wake up while I was gone. Taking the melatonin out of my purse, I shook three tablets into my hand and went over to the bed where Sage was still sleeping. I put the tablets in his mouth because eventually they would dissolve and he would swallow the saliva that would form in his mouth. Then his ass would sleep until the next day.

Grabbing my keys off the dresser, I slung the purse strap over my shoulder and left the room. It took about twenty minutes to arrive at Lady Loves. The line was long as hell and I wasn't trying to stand in it alongside some of the bum bitches I saw in attendance.

After parking my car down the street, I walked back to the club and straight to the front of the line.

"Whoa, do you see the line right there? Get in it!" the bouncer at the door barked.

"You gon' get your ass kicked if I have to call my brother out here. He wouldn't like the way you're talking to his sister. As a matter of fact, let me give Dap a call right now." I pulled my phone from my purse and dude's eyes bucked as I fake dialed on the key-pad.

"Nah, my bad, ma. Go ahead and go in. I don't want no smoke."

He opened the door for me to walk through and I blended in with the patrons that were inside. The atmosphere was crazy and the music was on point. I turned towards VIP and spotted Wes standing close to the railing choppin' it up with some dude. I needed to dis-appear so I could watch him without being seen. An empty stool at the bar was where I headed and I had the perfect view to Wes watch.

"If you're going to sit here, you must buy a drink. Otherwise, you have to get up."

I looked at the bartender and smirked. If I wasn't trying to be inconspicuous, her ass would've gotten read. But keeping my cool, I decided to just order a drink. She had dodged a bullet, but I dared her to try that shit a second time.

"Let me get a Long Island iced tea," I said, throwing a ten-dollar bill on the counter. There was a group of white dudes standing off to the side of the bar and they were talking while watching Dap's VIP section.

"This black bastard is living it up off my money," the tallest one gritted. "If he thinks I'm leaving without what's rightfully belongs to me, he's out of his mind.

"Kalene, were you able to talk to the son of a bitch?" a younger dude asked.

"Luciano, barely. He's mad because I left his ass without any explanations, but give me time and I will get him to talk to me. Dap still loves me. There's no way he will continue to turn me away."

I didn't even know the bitch was with the group of guys because she was sitting at the bar cool as fuck. My ears perked up knowing

I wasn't the only one out to disrupt the King's lives. The bartender placed my drink in front of me and I had just raised the straw to my mouth when I was bumped from behind, causing my drink to splash on the front of my dress. Spinning around angrily, I came face to face with Wes' wife.

"Oh, my bad," she said, patting my shoulder.

"No problem. It's all good," I replied nicely since she didn't recognize me. The Kalene chick peeked over her shoulder as Justice walked through the crowd.

"That's his brother's bitch. I thought she was with Dap, but found out that wasn't the case before he told me to leave his section."

"Bene, aggiungeremo il suo culo al nostro gioco per arrivare a suo cognato poi." (well, we will add her ass to our game to get at her brother-in-law then).

I didn't know what language he was speaking, but they looked like they were part of some type of mafia. Dap was in some type of shit and I didn't want no parts of it. The way Luciano was eyeing Justice had me thinking he had a plan stirring in his mind for her.

"Oh shit, they are looking this way," Kalene said, jumping off the stool and blending into the crowd.

I turned around and the entire section was making their way down the stairs in a hurry. The front entrance was a no go because I would have to pass the stairs, so I opted to take plan B. Sliding from the stool quickly, I pushed my way through the crowd of people, keeping my eyes on the red exit sign. There was no way I could allow them to get my ass because I wasn't ready to die.

I pushed the emergency door and the alarm went off. I kicked off my shoes and took off running. I heard the door slamming against the brick wall, but I was hauling ass like a track star and bent the corner fast. I hit the button on the key fob that I removed from the side pocket of my purse. I was in the driver's seat in record time and started the car as I saw Wes round the very corner I had just vacated. Wasting no time, I threw the car in drive and took off, running straight through a red light.

It was just my luck the police were nowhere in sight because I would've gotten pulled the fuck over. I jumped on I-94 and sped all the way back to the suburbs to get as far away from the club as possible. My phone rang and I shuffled around in my purse without taking my eyes off the road. I answered without looking at the screen and I wished I hadn't done so.

"Hello?"

"Bitch, you got away this time. But you got until noon tomorrow to drop my son off at a fire station, hospital, police station, or my muthafuckin' house! If I have to come looking for you, the suffering I'm gon' make you go through will be hell!"

Wes ended the call before I could say anything in return. I kept blinking like I had Tourette's syndrome and I was nervous as hell. Wes sounded like the devil himself on the phone and I had to come up with another plan fast.

Chapter 12

Sage

My mommy told Auntie Nell not to leave me by myself and that's all she had been doing since she took me from Beverly's house. When she left me and thought I was sleeping, I laid in the bed and faked it. She put the candy in my mouth, but I spit it out when she turned her back to get her purse. Those candies made me go to sleep all the time and I was tired of sleeping. The only thing I wanted to do was go home to my mama.

Auntie Nell left and I got out of bed and ran to the window. I remembered the numbers and letters on the car and ran to the table to write them on a piece of paper. Auntie Nell was not the same person she was when I was little. She was mean now and she hit me. Mommy only took my things away for a while, but she never hit me.

I picked up the phone, pushed my mommy's number, and waited for her to answer. She didn't answer so I listened for the beep the way she taught me and started talking like I would if she was on the phone. "Mommy, it's me, Sage. Come get me. Auntie Nell left me by myself again and I don't know where she is. I'm in a room that just got a bed in it and we went on a long car ride too."

A loud buzzing sound came through the phone and I hung up. The clothes Auntie Nell took off me, I put them back on, and my shoes too. She couldn't make me stay by myself no more. I was going to find my mommy. It's been a long time since I saw her and I miss Beverly, my new uncle Wes, and Donovan too. They were funny to me and I wanted to see them.

I walked to the door putting my coat on and took my hat out of the pocket. I looked back at the phone and thought I should try calling Mommy one more time. After dialing her number again, a man answered the phone and I didn't care if it wasn't Mommy, it was somebody.

"Hello?" I didn't say nothing so the man spoke again. "Who is this? Shanell?"

"No, it's Sage. Auntie Nell not here. Where's my mommy? Tell her she has to come get me."

"Sage, this is Grandpa Wes. Where are you?"

"I don't know. Auntie Nell took me and we went on a long ride and she kept giving me candy that made me sleepy. I'm scared because she screams and hits me," I said, starting to cry.

"Don't cry, Sage. Everything will be alright. Okay, listen to me. Look around and see if you see something with the name of the hotel on it. Look for the word hotel or motel. H-O-T-E-L."

My new grandpa was talking to me like I was slow, but I let him think he was great because I was smart to be five. I found a card by the phone and it said Hiat (Hyatt) hotel and I got happy.

"I found something! I'm at the Hiat hotel," I told him.

"Okay, there should be an address on there too. Read me what it says. If you can't, spell it out."

"I'm going to spell everything. Write it down, grandpa. Hurry, because Auntie Nell might be coming back soon."

"Give me the address, Sage."

"H-Y-A-T-T, R-E-G-E-N-C-Y, H-O-T-E-L. 1800 E Golf, I know that word from school!"

"That's good, son. Tell me the rest," Grandpa said.

"R-O-A-D, S-C-H-A-U-M-B-U-R-G, I-L," I finished reading off what I saw on the card.

"Got it. This is what I need you to do. I'm about fifteen minutes away and I'm coming to get you. How long has Shanell been gone?"

"Not too long, but she had on a dress so she probably went on a date."

"Open the door and tell me what room you are in." I put the phone down and ran to the door. There was a number by the door.

"319, 319, 319," I said over and over as I closed and locked the door. "It's 319," I repeated into the phone.

"Okay, I'm almost there I will knock on the door four times and you will know it's me. Put your coat on and wait for me. Don't leave that room until I get there, Sage."

"What if Auntie Nell comes back?"

"I'll take care of her if she does. Are you alright, Sage?"

"No, I'm not. I didn't have a chance to tell Beverly I was going with Auntie Nell. I hope she's not mad at me. The only reason I went was because Auntie Nell told me she was taking me to my mommy. But she didn't. We were driving a long time and I don't know where we went." Grandpa was quiet and I thought he hung up the phone. "Hello? You still there?"

"Yeah, I'm here, Sage. Beverly's not mad at you."

"Good, because I want to tell her I'm sorry for leaving. Is my tablet still at her house? I need to call Olivia on video because I miss her."

My grandpa laughed. "Who is Olivia, Sage?"

"She's my girlfriend. I'm gonna ask Uncle Wes and Uncle Dap to talk to her daddy so she can be my wife. He's trying to keep me away from Olivia, but it's not happening. I don't have a daddy, but I have two uncles and they're bigger than him too. Are you almost here?" I asked, getting scared that Auntie Nell would come back before he got to me.

There were four knocks on the door and my eyes got big. "Is that you, Grandpa?" I whispered into the phone.

"Come open the door, Sage," he said hanging up the phone.

Doing as I was told, I hung up the phone before going to open the door. I hugged my grandpa and he picked me up. I buried my head in his neck. He had me happy to be leaving that room. Auntie Nell was evil.

"Thank you for coming to get me. Now you have to keep Auntie Nell from coming to get me. She is going to be so mad."

"Don't worry about that. Let's go see your mommy and get you something to eat," he said, walking away from the room with me in his arms.

Meesha

Chapter 13

Wes

Justice rushed up to me and whispered that Shanell was in the club and I jumped up quickly. Dap followed suit and the rest of the niggas fell in line. Locking eyes with the bitch, I pushed any and everything in my path out of my way. She tore ass out of the emergency doors and was able to jump in her car, peeling away.

"Damn, the bitch ran like a crackhead who stole a pack," Dap laughed as we watched the back of the car disappear down the street.

I didn't think the shit was funny at all. Shanell was lucky because I would've choked her until she took her last breath. Instead, I pulled out my phone and dialed her number. Listening as the phone rang, she answered in a shaky voice.

"Hello?"

"Bitch, you got away this time. But you got until noon tomorrow to drop my son off at a fire station, hospital, police station, or my muthafuckin' house! If I have to come looking for you, the suffering I'm gon' make you go through will be hell!" Ending the call, I stormed toward the front of the club with Dap behind me.

"My nigga is back! It took long enough for you to come out of hiding. I'm glad you're back. I know you peeped them Italian niggas that were standing next to the bar, right?"

"What? Nah, the only person I saw was Shanell's walking dead ass. Running scared ass bitch!"

"Rocco's sons were in that muthafucka, but I acted like I didn't see 'em. They gon' try to come for a nigga and I'll be ready for 'em," Dap said as we neared the entrance to the club.

There was a crowd of people out front and I spotted Dap's boy Juice getting pushed back by a big ass Italian dude in a tailor-made suit. "Ain't that yo' guy, brah?" I asked, picking up my pace.

"Hell yeah! What the fuck going on?" The both of us rushed toward the crowd, pushing our way through.

"Lucci, I will blow yo' muthafuckin' head off right here!" Juice screamed. "Man, get the fuck off me! This bitch ain't about to be talking all this shit, throwing threats around like he can't be touched! I don't give a damn who he is!"

"Let him go, Martino, he straight," Dap said, walking up to Juice. "Pipe down, fam. I'm who this muthafucka lookin' for."

"Dap, all I want is what belongs to me. Sign over both stores and this can be over," Luciano yelled out.

"You must me out of your mind, fool! I'm not signing over shit. Customs belongs to me! I worked my ass off to get it where it is today. Maybe if yo' bum ass quit snorting all your money away, you can do something with yourself. Blood, sweat, and tears is how you become successful. Not always waiting for a handout."

"Let's settle this once and for all, Dap. We all know you're good with your guns. Let's see how good you are with those hands." Luciano took off his suit jacket, dropping it to the ground.

"Walk away while you can, Lucci. You ain't no match for me, son," Dap laughed.

The crowd opened up and Luciano walked through the middle in Dap's direction. Christian stepped in front of him and put his hand up to stop Luciano from coming forward. Luciano looked up at his uncle with a menacing glare, but that didn't move Christian at all.

"Don't stop him, Chris. Let him through so I can fuck him up the way my daddy used to do me growing up. He hasn't had nothing but a silver spoon in his mouth all his life. I'm about to show him what street life really feels like."

Standing front and center, I watched everything going on because wasn't nobody going to call themselves jumpin' my brother. Even though I knew Dap was about to beat the fuck out of dude, I still wanted to make sure it was one on one.

Luciano, or whatever his name was, walked up with his fist up. Dap let him get close and swung from downtown. He knocked his head back hard enough to hear the kinks pop out of his neck. There was a lot of "damns" and "oh shits" from the crowd. One of his boys tried to come for Dap and Christian shook his head slowly at him.

"Get back in there, Lucci. This is what you wanted, right? Take that shit like a man and prove yourself.

90

"Fuck you, Christian!" he said, wiping the blood from his lip. "That shit was soft."

"Shid, your neck told a different story, nigga," Dap laughed.

Luciano charged him. Dap caught his ass with an uppercut and he stumble back. Recovering quickly, he swung and connected his fist with Dap's jaw. Truthfully, I believe bro let him get that hit in because he went in on his ass. No mercy. Luciano was swinging wildly, but wasn't connecting at all.

When Dap went in on his ribcage, out of my peripheral, I saw one of his boys rush to jump in. He was yanked back forcefully and he turned around with rage in his eyes, but stopped when he came face to face with Justice's Nine. He smirked at her and I took a step in their direction when my wife drew back and smacked his ass on the side of the head.

"Nigga, you got the right one tonight. That's a fair mutha-fuckin' fight! If he gets his ass beat, so be it."

"Bitch!" he screamed, looking at the blood on his fingers.

Justice took a step back and cocked her tool and pointed it at his chest. "You thought that was supposed to move me? Nigga, you don't want this hot shit in yo' ass. Please don't let my sexy fool you. I'll send yo' ass back to Cali in a muthafuckin' box!"

The sound of sirens rang out. "Break this shit up!" one of the officers said into a bullhorn.

My eyes never left Justice. I watched as she quickly slipped away while putting her gun back in place under her dress. She held her own and I was proud of her for that shit, even though I was pissed because she should've left that shit for us to handle.

"That's enough, Dap. Let him go," Christian said, separating him and Luciano. "You have too much to lose. Get out of here."

Dap wiped at his shirt while grinning at Luciano. "You finished, Lucci? Are you gon' leave this shit alone? Or are you gon' get yo' ass whooped again? It's up to you, fam. Just know I'll be ready when you pull up again."

"I'll be done when I get what's mine," he shot back.

"I guess you better find a boxing gym, shooting range, or something, because you gon' need that shit." Reaching in his pocket, Dap peeled off a couple bills and tossed them at his feet. "Go to Walgreens and get you some shit to patch up them wounds. Don't forget the Epsom salt. You need to soak when you get to your hotel, your body is about to hurt all over, nigga."

Justice walked to my side and I grabbed her hand and followed Dap to valet. As we waited for our cars, the same female from the club came walking up the street. She looked worried, but Dap was looking down at his hand and didn't see her coming our way.

"Hey, bro, here comes your girl," I said lowly. Looking up, his eyes squinted as he watched her approach.

She glanced at me then at Justice before she said anything. "Are you alright?" she asked, addressing Dap.

"It don't matter, Kalene. Why are you over here?" he asked, folding his arms over his chest.

"You don't have to be so mean, Donovan."

At that moment, our cars were brought out and Dap moved to step off the curb. Kalene grabbed his forearm, stopping him.

"If you don't get your fuckin' hands off me! Go wherever you're going, Kalene, before you make me embarrass yo' ass out here. Walk away like you did in California," he said, heading to his car. "Bro, I'll get up with you tomorrow. We have to go to Pops' house in the afternoon."

"Aight, bet. Drive safely, man," I said, opening the door for Justice. As I walked to the driver's door, Dap drove off in his BMW and a white Lamborghini pulled out behind him.

Jumping in the car, I knew something was about to go down and I had to be there for my brother. I pulled away from the curb and bent the same corner Dap did. I saw him up ahead and pushed the Range to seventy trying to catch up with him. When I got closer, his stupid ass was pulling over.

"Don't get out of that car, Dap," I said out loud.

The Lamborghini slowed down before getting to his car. I swerved in the oncoming lane and there weren't any cars coming, so I kept going. Lifting the armrest, I grabbed my bitch and cocked it. Justice's window went down and I noticed for the first time she had her Nine in her hand. The Lambo pulled up beside Dap's car and I pulled up to it and my wife let her bitch sing.

Pow, pow, pow!

She hit the driver in the head. The passenger turned around and was shot in the back of the head by Dap. The bullet came out of his forehead and entered the driver's neck. Dap sped off and I was right on his ass. A muthafucka had to wake up early to catch a King in a helpless situation. The heat was going to pick up after this shit for sure.

***

There was nothing said as I drove the twenty minutes home. When Dap turned off at his exit, I kept going, checking the rearview mirror to make sure no other car got off with him. Taking the next exit, I made a right turn and drove down the street to my crib. I threw the truck in park, then turned to Justice before attempting to get out.

"What were you thinking when you shot into that car, Justice?"

She looked at me like I was a stranger to her. Unbuckling her seatbelt, Justice turned her whole body around in the seat and glared at me for a moment. "First of all, I had to make the move because by the time you got out of this truck, they would've lit your ass up! Second of all, I was right there and couldn't give them the opportunity to kill your brother! Don't question me when I was looking out the way I was supposed to. I'm not the type of bitch that's about to watch shit unfold!"

Justice was mad as hell as she climbed out of the truck, slammed the door, and stalked toward the house. Snatching the key from the ignition, I followed quickly because I didn't appreciate how she snapped and got out. Nah, this shit was far from over. When I entered the house, my wife was climbing the stairs.

"Bring yo' ass back down here, Justice!"

"You got me fucked up, Weston King," she snapped, turning on the step she was standing on. "Do I look like Shanell to you? You have never used that tone with me and you won't start now. I understand everything that's been going on has reverted you back to the street nigga you were, but the way you're speaking to me is going to take me back to the same streets I vacated too."

"Shit, I've already seen it with my own eyes. Justice, I don't want you to fall victim to the street. You are a mother and a wife now," I said, bringing my voice down.

"I grew up a victim to the streets. I just put it behind me. What was the use of having my gun if I wasn't going to use it?"

"I get it, okay? Make that your last time pulling a gun and not using it. I'm referring to back at the club."

"Wes, you weren't watching good enough. I didn't have to shoot his ass. I left his ass leaking for a bunch of niggas to see and the police showed up at the right time. If I had pulled the trigga, I'd be locked the fuck up right now. You talking real stupid right now. I'm starting to question if Corporate America has made you softer than a marshmallow."

"So, me trying to protect my wife is wrong?"

"I'm not saying that. Just know I will never leave home without my piece and I will use this bitch again if I have to. Hopefully I catch your crazy-ass ex on the street. I'll take a charge for that bitch any day. She is going down for old and new, so get mad now."

She turned and continued up the stairs. I shook my head and went into the kitchen to grab something to eat. About ten minutes later, Justice was walking down the stairs in a pair of black leggings, a green T-shirt, and green Chucks to match. After getting her down coat from the closet, Justice snatched her keys from the island, but I stopped her before she got to the door.

"Where are you going?" I asked.

"I'm going to get my baby, if that's alright with you," she replied, rolling her eyes.

"Not alone you're not. Give me a minute and we will go together. Don't go out that door, Justice. I'm serious."

"Hurry up, because I'm ready to go to sleep."

I slapped mayo on my ham sandwich and placed it on a napkin before making my way out the door. Justice opened the door with force and stomped down the steps to her car. I turned to lock the door and before I could turn around, she was backing out of the driveway. I'd never wanted to choke her ass before, but I swear the image was in my mind vividly at the moment.

Jumping in my truck, I backed out of the driveway and sped down the street to Dap's crib. When I pulled up, Justice was standing at the door and it opened as I parked. I sat finishing off my sandwich before opening the door. I took a deep breath and stepped out as my brother waited for me on the porch.

"Why the fuck y'all come over here in separate cars?" Dap asked.

"Justice has a whole attitude because I got in her ass about pulling her gun. I could've handled that shit," I said as I walked up the steps.

"Brah, she did what she had to do. Wasn't nobody trying to wait for them niggas to bust first. You would've had to shoot over her to hit your target. I get that you didn't want her to shoot, but it was necessary. Take it easy on her. One thing I can say, she handled her muthafuckin' business. Justice was bustin' that thang right along with me and she hit they ass with precision too."

"I don't need her out here being a gangsta bitch, Dap! Faith needs her."

"That's true, but you also know with all the shit going on, she has to stay ready. At least you know sis can take care of herself. That's a great attribute to have," he said, turning to go into the house.

As we entered, Justice was in the middle of telling Tana what transpired at the club. Their eyes fell upon us and Justice stopped talking. "Keep going; there's nothing to hide," Dap said taking a seat on the barstool.

"So are we going to have a problem with this Kalene bitch?" Tana asked with her feet tucked under her on the couch.

"Nah, I told you a little bit about her before. I'm still trying to figure out why she was at the event to begin with. There's nothing going on with Kalene and things were over when she left me high and dry back in California. Reconnecting with her is something I have no intention of doing. You are my woman, Tana. Another woman would never be able to take me away from you and our unborn child. You have my word on that."

I'd never heard Dap express himself to a woman before. Tana was the one for him, but I knew Kalene was trying to get back into his life for a reason. I just hoped she went back to the west coast after the way Dap curved her ass at the club.

"Well, maybe we can learn a little bit more about her soon. Trust is a huge part of being with someone and I have to put that in action. Now, if you violate me in anyway, it's game over. I'm not for giving second chances. I've been through too much to deal with any more bullshit."

"Tana, I'm nothing like the nigga that did you dirty. I want you to concentrate on the way I treat you versus what you're used to. Tyson's ass is on borrowed time anyway, so he's irrelevant.

Dap stood to his feet and moved until he was in front of Tana. Lifting her from the couch, he hugged her tightly and kissed her sensually on the lips. Dap took a step back and caressed the Queen of Customs Charm that he had given her.

"No other woman has received anything of this magnitude from me. This may be material shit to you, but it's everything to me. Before you became pregnant, I chose you as my better half. These words have never meant so much to me ever in life as they do right now. Montana, I love you. Nothing could ever come between what we have."

I stood back in awe because I had never heard Donovan King profess his love to any woman in the manner he had that night. His words were sincere and I believed him. I didn't know what Tana had done to my brother, but she had his heart in the palm of her hands.

"Kalene ain't shit to me! You are the one I care about. Fuck what another bitch is trying to do because she won't get far with whatever she has planned. I shut that shit down at the door."

"It's good to know you didn't indulge in the bullshit. I'm not worried about her; I was worried about how you responded to the situation. My problem would never be with Kalene. It would be solely on you. I love you too and we will continue to grow stronger together."

"That's my plan, baby. To grow together. I want you by my side forever, Tana," Dap said, kissing her tenderly. He turned to Justice and smirked.

"Sis, thank you for bossin' up on them niggas! It was very impressive. As you saw, I was gunnin' for their ass too. You were quick with yo' shit and I appreciate that. Wes don't want you in these streets and he has every right to think the way he does. I don't want y'all arguing over something that wasn't preventable. You did what you had to do."

"I'm not arguing with him, Dap. One thing my husband's not going to do is talk to me like I'm new to this shit. If the shoe was on the other foot, I would've been gun blazing for his ass too. There are too many things to worry about with Shanell, and now we got other shit to worry about with these weak-ass Italians. If I have to pull out again, I will."

Looking at my wife stand on her actions, I couldn't even be mad at her any longer. I didn't have to like it, but I would respect it long as she didn't go out looking for the bullshit that was going on. The husband in me wanted to snatch her ass up and demand that she took a seat somewhere, but deep inside, I knew I couldn't do any of the sort.

"Justice, I apologize for raising my voice at you. As your husband, it's my job to protect you and our daughter. I can't do that if you are trying to be the nigga in this marriage. I've stressed what I wanted from you but the urge to pull the trigga is back in your soul. All I ask is that you are careful when you are out."

Faith started wailing loudly and Justice headed up the stairs without replying to what I had said to her. There was no talking to her. My wife was going to do whatever was necessary if it came her way.

When she came back downstairs, Faith was bundled up and ready to go. Saying our goodbyes to Dap and Tana, we left to go home as a family.

Meesha

Chapter 14

Wes Sr.

When I went to the hotel and rescued Sage, taking him to the hospital ended up being a bust because I couldn't get in with him. Instead, I took him back to my house and while I was hesitant to go inside, Sage was eager to see Beverly. I didn't know how to tell him that his grandma would never grace our home again.

"What are you waiting for, Grandpa? I want to see Grandma Bev," Sage said, standing up with his head between the front seats.

"Sage, Grandma Bev isn't inside, I said sadly. "I'll explain it to you tomorrow. Right now, I want to get you inside and get you something to eat. We also have to call your mommy."

"Okay, that sounds good because I'm so hungry. Auntie Nell didn't feed me before she left. Do you think she's going to come here to try to get me again?"

"No. Shanell knows not to come to my house. You are safe with me, Sage. You don't have to worry about your Auntie Nell anymore."

I opened the driver's door and got out. Walking around to open the door for Sage, I watched him hop out of the back and waited for me to lead the way up the walkway. When I unlocked the door, the smell of my wife filled the entryway heavily and my heart started pumping because it made me hope Bev would come walking out of the kitchen. But it didn't happen and I was crushed.

The thought of living without the one woman that put up with all of my bullshit for almost thirty years was tough. All of my infidelities came back full throttle and I felt guilty that I didn't cherish my wife through the duration of our marriage. Even though she forgave me years before, I still felt like the scum of the earth because I took her for granted.

"Sage, would you like a turkey sandwich?" I asked, walking to the kitchen after locking up and setting the alarm.

"Can I have Cocoa Pebbles instead?" he asked.

"You can have whatever you want, buddy."

"I'll have cereal. I only want some because I haven't had any since I was last here." Sage happily ran to the kitchen table and climbed in the nearest chair as I prepared his cereal.

Once I set the bowl of chocolatey cereal in front of my grandson, he dug right in, just like Bria used to do when she was younger. I laughed at the sight before me because Sage looked like a replica of Wes, but he had the mannerisms of Bria. Knowing he was Wes' son caused me to step back and take in his features. At almost six years old, it was going to be hard to explain to Sage that Bria was his aunt and not his mother. Hopefully the transition wasn't going to be too hard for him.

Sage lifted the bowl to his lips and I knew he was about finished with his cereal. I'd never let my children eat cereal for dinner, but I guess this was life when you became a grandparent. I took out my phone and Facetimed Bria. Waiting for her to answer, I sat in the chair beside Sage and waited patiently for the line to connect. When Bria finally answered, her eyes were puffy and her nose was red.

"Did you get him, Daddy?" were the first words out of her mouth.

"Yes, baby. I got him."

"Mommy!" Sage squealed, hopping out of the chair at the sound of Bria's voice and rushed to my side. "Why are you in the hospital?" he asked, peering at the screen.

"Mommy has a little boo. I'll be back to you soon."

"Is Grandma Bev there with you? I want to see her," Sage pouted.

"No, she's not here."

Bria's voice cracked and tears ran down her face rapidly at the mention of Beverly. I had to cut in before she revealed the truth I knew would shatter Sage's little heart. I wanted Wes to be in attendance when I broke the news to him about Beverly's death.

"Sage, I told you we would talk about Grandma Beverly tomorrow. Tell your mommy goodnight so you can get ready for bed. We have to get up early so you can see her in the morning."

"I can't tell her goodnight while she's crying. I'm always there when Mommy isn't feeling good, Grandpa. We all we got," Sage said sternly. "Mommy, please stop crying. Everything will be alright. I'll be there bright and early in the morning to kiss your pain away, just like you did when I scraped my knee."

"I know, baby. Go brush your teeth and get ready for bed. I'll see you when you get here. I love you so much, Sage. Don't you ever forget that, okay?" Bria forced a smile to assure Sage that she was alright even though she was hurting inside.

"I love you too, Mommy. No more crying," he said, blowing her a kiss. "I'm going to bed now and yes; I'll make sure to brush my teeth and say my prayers. Goodnight."

Sage went back to his bowl and picked it up, walking it to the sink. He was so mature for his age and I was proud of the mother Bria was to him. Sage walked past me and doubled back, giving me a hug before he exited the kitchen. I listened as his little feet scurried up the stairs and became a distant memory.

"Daddy, did Shanell hurt my baby?" Bria asked as she wiped her eyes.

"No. Sage is perfectly fine. The only thing I can actually say is, Shanell lost all trust with that little boy. He said she hit him and kept giving him candy that made him sleepy. When I find her, she's going to die, Bria. Your old man may be spending the rest of his life in prison."

The tears that stung my eyes escaped the minute I blinked. "There's no way she can get away with killing your mother. She took a part of me away."

"Daddy, please don't do anything drastic. Shanell is going to get caught by that bitch named karma. God don't like ugly and he's not too fond of pretty."

"There's nothing you or anyone else can say to convince me to spare her life. I have nothing else to live for."

"Stop talking like that, please. You still have me, Wes, Dap, and Sage to live for. Beverly wouldn't want you to throw your life away. I'm so sorry for contributing to Shanell's madness. I didn't know she was going to take it this far."

"Don't you dare blame yourself for what she has done! You played your part because she forced you to do so. Never let anyone manipulate you into doing anything that stupid again, Bria. The way this family looks out for one another should've had you running to us the minute you found out what was going on. Instead, you let your emotions lead you into a trap that almost cost you your life."

"I'm sorry, Daddy," Bria cried. "If I had told, none of this would've happened."

"That's not necessarily true. Everything happens for a reason and Shanell's unstable. She would've found a way to get back at Wes regardless. Get some rest. I'm going upstairs to check on Sage and try to get some sleep myself. I love you, baby girl."

"I love you too, Daddy. Did you tell Wes that you got Sage back?"

"Nah, I'm going to call him once I'm off the phone with you. I got this, Bria. I'll see you bright and early in the morning, like Sage said. I know he's going to be the first to wake up, dressed and ready to go. Is there anything you need me to bring for you?"

"Yes, some real food. I want French toast, eggs with cheese, and some orange juice."

"Anything for you, baby girl. Goodnight and I love you, Bria."

"I love you too, Daddy," Bria said, ending the call.

After turning off the lights and checking the alarm, I walked slowly up the stairs and went directly toward the room Sage was in. Outside the door, I could hear his small voice on the other side and I listened closely to make out what he was saying. It was kind of difficult because his voice was so soft.

"God, I need a favor. Mommy taught me to pray for other people as well as myself. But I need you to give me strength to hold my new family together. Something bad happened and the grownups thinks I'm slow to what's really going on. No one will tell me where my grandma Bev is, but I have a feeling she's no longer on this earth with us." I was shocked to hear him say that and wondered how he came to the conclusion without really knowing us as a family.

"Grandpa won't tell me where she is and Mommy's eyes shifted when I asked about Grandma Bev. She does that when she's trying not to tell me the honest truth. I just want someone to tell me where

Grandma Bev is. If she's there with you, Lord, please tell her I love her and she will always be in my heart. In Jesus' name, amen."

Sage was too observant for his age, but I knew there was no way I could continue to keep him in the dark. Lightly pecking on the door with my knuckle, I gave Sage the respect of allowing me to enter. I listened as he shuffled around a bit, then he finally called out for me to come in. As I stepped inside the room, Sage was lying on his back staring at the ceiling.

"Are you okay, son?" I asked, sitting on the edge of the bed.

"No. Can I ask you a question, Grandpa?"

"Sage, you can ask me anything." I sat quietly, waiting on him to ask whatever his little heart desired.

Sitting up and propping a pillow behind him, Sage took a deep breath and turned his head towards me. "Tell me the truth, grandpa. Where is Grandma Bev?"

"Sage, I heard you praying and I think you already have an idea where Beverly is. You are young and may not understand—"

"I understand more than you give me credit for, Grandpa. Did Auntie Nell kill Grandma Bev? Tell me the truth. I'm a kid, but I know something happened the day she took me from the yard next door."

I lowered my head as I cleared my throat. "Yes, Sage. Your grandma Bev transitioned the day Shanell kidnapped you. Her homegoing will be next week and I want you to understand that she is in a better place. Beverly may not be here with us in flesh—"

"But she will always be in our hearts," Sage finished the saying with me. "I have one more question before I go to sleep. Did you tell Wes that you have me here with you?"

"I'm going to call him and Donovan in a few," I responded.

"Uncle Donovan is cool and I like him a lot. Getting to know him better is going to be so much fun. Does Wes know he's my daddy?"

That revelation took me by surprise and my voice was caught in my throat. My mind wandered back to the day I brought Sage and Bria to the house and vividly pictured him sitting at the table with his headphones on at the dinner table. His little ass heard everything that was said about the subject.

"Wes knows you are his, son, but he just recently learned the truth. Sage, I don't want you to blame him for not being in your life. He didn't know you existed. How do you feel knowing Bria is your aunt and not your mother?"

"She will always be my mommy! Shanell will never be a mother to me! I hate her, Grandpa! I hate her!" Sage wailed loudly.

Embracing Sage in my arms, I let him cry himself to sleep before lying him back on the pillow and covering his body with the sheet. Easing out of the room quietly, I dialed Wes' number and waited for him to answer. The call went to voicemail and I ended the call without leaving a message.

I placed the phone on my bed and removed my clothes, throwing everything in the hamper as I entered the bathroom. I turned the shower on and took a leak before stepping under the hot water. My eyes closed and my beautiful wife was standing in front of me with a wide smile on her face. Tears ran down my face and the water washed them away quickly as they fell.

My emotions were all over the place. I was happy to see Beverly's face again, but it was replaced with sadness knowing the only way I would be able to see her were at times like the one I was having at that moment. Fear set in and I wondered how was I going to live without the love of my life. My emotions changed to anger quickly when I thought about how she was taken away from me.

After washing my body thoroughly with my eyes closed the entire time, I turned the water off and stood admiring my wife. "I will always love you, Beverly King. I'm so sorry I wasn't there to protect you. Avenging your death is my top priority. I put that on my life," I said out loud.

Knock, knock, knock.

"Pops are you in there?" Wes' voice rang out, causing me to let my wife go as I opened my eyes and stepped out of the shower. Wrapping a towel around my waist, I opened the door and the steam followed me into my bedroom. "I've been calling you since you called my phone. I'm sorry I didn't answer. I didn't hear my phone ring."

"It's okay," I said, throwing a T-shirt over my head. Walking into my closet, I slipped on a pair of basketball shorts before emerging back into the room.

"What's going on?" Wes asked.

"I found Sage."

"Where is he? Did Shanell bring him back here? What happened?" Wes asked question after question without giving me an opportunity to respond.

"He's in the guest bedroom next to mine. Sage called Bria's phone and I answered. He helped me locate him after Shanell left him in a hotel room alone. Once Sage gave me the address he found on a card in the room, I went to get him. Sage did the right thing reaching out for help. There's no telling what that bitch would've done to him."

"She left my son in a fuckin' hotel room by himself at five years old while she came to the fuckin' club to shake her ass! Shanell is lucky she got away, but there's only so many times a snake can slither through the cracks. I won't stop until she's taking a dirt bath after all she's done to this family." Wes turned to leave the room.

"Son, wait a minute. Sage knows your mother is dead and he also knows you are his father. I didn't tell him; he already knew. Sage cried himself to sleep before I got in the shower. Leave him be until the morning. We are going to the hospital to see Bria. I think it would be best that you are there when Bria explains everything about not being his mother."

"I'll be there. I won't miss another day of Sage's life. I was already robbed of damn near six years. Pops, shit is hard for you right now. The last thing I want you to do is wallow in pain. If you need me, don't hesitate to call. I will be here for you whenever you need me to be. I've never seen you cry, but there's evidence that you've been doing just that tonight. I love you, old man, and I'm here."

"Wes, I don't know how to go on without your mother. Saying goodbye to her is going to be hard. Life will never be the same. I don't think I want to have a service, son. Seeing her in that state is something I won't be able to do."

"Pops, we will talk about it tomorrow when we meet up here with Uncle Spencer. I love you. Get some rest. Do you want me to stay the night?"

"No, son. Go home to your family. I'll be alright, I promise. I can't do anything drastic because Sage is in the house. A drink won't hurt anything though," I said, drawing my son into a hug. "I love you too, Junior. You have to tell me all about the party later. Watch yourself out there. Shanell is plotting."

Wes peeked in on Sage before we made our way downstairs. When he left, I had a couple shots of Bacardi Gold before I went upstairs and passed out.

Chapter 15

Tana

I was sitting in the house while Dap went to conduct business at Customs. The store was bringing in a lot of business and the money was rolling in at a rapid pace. When Dap asked me to look over his books, I couldn't turn him down. It was boring sitting in the house all the time after the bullshit Tyson pulled.

Beverly's homegoing was in a few days and no one was looking forward to facing the task. Wes Sr. didn't want to have a service at first, but with a little bit of convincing from Wes and Dap, he decided to go through with it. Truth be told, I believed he made the right choice because he had to say his final farewell in order to cope with Beverly being gone.

Grabbing my phone after completing the last of the input with the Custom accounts, I called Justice. She answered the phone immediately.

"What's up, bestie? How you doing over there?"

"I'm tired of being in this house. I want to go out for a little while. Ask your father-in-law if he can watch Faith while we go out and get some fresh air."

"Faith can roll with us. I'll have to call Wes and tell him we are heading out. I think you should tell Dap as well. I'm not trying to hear shit about you leaving without letting him know. He has been on your ass like white on rice lately."

"I'm grown, Jus! I don't have to check in with him."

"That's not what I'm saying at all, Tana. It's the right thing to do, bestie. We don't know when Tyson will show up. He's been really quiet since he violated you. Plus, you are carrying that man's child, in case you forgot."

"How can I forget, Justice? I'm reminded every time I'm hovering over the toilet for no reason at all," I said, rolling my eyes. "I'm about to call him now. You happy?"

"Yes, I am, ma'am," Justice laughed. "Handle your business and Faith and I will be there soon." Ending the call with Justice, I hit Dap's name and listened as the phone rang. He finally answered at the tail end of the last ring.

"Tana. Hey baby, how you doing?"

"I'm fine. I wanted you to know, I'm going out with Justice and Faith."

"Tana, you and Justice don't need to be out alone. I'm wrapped up with Customs and Wes is getting some last minute things together with Pops. There's too much going on right now. It's not a good time."

"Dap, I'm not worried about anything happening. I'm tired of sitting in this house. My face is cleared up, for the most part, and I'm ready to get back to life. I can't let what happened to me stifle my movements."

"I'm worried, Montana! You are carrying my child and I don't want anything to happen to you!"

"Stop raising your voice at me, Donovan King! It's not necessary," I shot back.

"I'm sorry, but y'all not going out alone. I'll have Juice come roll with y'all. That's the only way," he said with finality.

"Whatever, Dap. Have him here within a half hour or I'm leaving with or without him."

"Leave that muthafucka without Juice and watch what happens to you, Tana. You have never had the beast unleashed on yo' ass, but you're pushing yo' luck! I'll see you when I get home, and I love yo' stubborn ass."

Without waiting for a reply from me, he hung up with an attitude. I wasn't worried about what he said. Instead, I went upstairs, took a quick shower, and got dressed. As I fluffed out my hair, the doorbell sounded and I rushed downstairs to let Justice and Faith in. Snatching the door open, I was taken aback when the man on the other side of the door stood with his arms crossed over his chest.

"You were never taught to ask who it is before opening the door?"

"Who the fuck is you?" I asked in return, ignoring his question.

"Hell, I could've been somebody that blew yo' shit back instantaneously with no problem if that's what I was on. You have to do better, ma. With the shit going on out here, you have to be cautious at all times. No wonder my nigga Dap wanted me to escort you where you wanted to go. You don't pay attention to shit!"

"Oh, you must be Juice," I said, smacking my lips. "Just so you know, I won't be riding with you. Justice and I will be rolling together."

"Nah, that's not what I was ordered to do. Dap told me to come escort you. Meaning, you are in the car with me. I'm not about to argue with you, ma. It's either that, or you stay your tough ass in this muthafuckin' house. Yo' choice."

"Well, stay your ass outside and guard the fort until I'm ready to leave. And watch how you speak to me too. I'm not the one to take too many orders from a stranger." Slamming the door in his face, I ran back upstairs and called Justice.

"What's up, Tana? What's taking you so long to come outside?" she asked.

"I didn't know you were here. I just closed the door in Dap's rinky dink ass security's face."

"I saw you," Justice laughed.

"How the hell did you see me? I didn't see your car outside."

"I'm in the back of Juice's truck. He came and picked me up from the house. Your phone should be ringing in three…two…one." Justice counted down and sure enough, Dap was calling on the other end.

"Hold on," I said as she laughed loudly in my ear. "Yes, Mr. King."

"Tana, what's wrong with you? Get in the car with Juice and mind your tongue, babe. You're starting to piss me off with this attitude of yours. You wanted to go out and I made it happen. Stop being so fuckin' bullheaded. The next time you snatch my door open without checking to see who's on the other side, we gon' fight."

"Tell your boy to watch how the hell he talks to me, and maybe I'll follow suit. You know I don't do well with disrespect. I gotta go and I'll see you later."

I hung up the phone, grabbed my coat, and made my way down stairs and out the door. Juice was still standing at the door with his back turned as he watched his truck like a hawk while waiting for me to make my exit. Pushing him slightly in the back so I could lock the door, he smirked and stepped forward just enough for me to handle my business. I made my way to the truck and once I was settled in the back seat with Justice, I stared at the back of Juice's head. I wanted to punch his ass.

"Where are y'all headed?" Juice asked.

"You know everything else. Why you don't know that?" I snapped.

"We are going to Ronnie's steakhouse downtown," Justice said, trying to keep the peace.

"Thank you, Miss Justice."

"You're welcome."

We rode in silence and the only sound in the truck was Justice giving Juice directions to the restaurant. We pulled up about twenty minutes later and went into the restaurant. We were seated immediately. Juice didn't come in with us, thank God. I didn't think I could contain myself from swinging on his ass if he had.

"Tana, you can straighten your face now," Justice chuckled. "Juice was only doing what he was told. You were two seconds from staying in the house. When he pulled out his phone, I knew he was telling on your ass."

"I don't give a fuck! Dap is not my daddy."

"I bet you don't be saying that shit when he in them guts," Justice laughed.

"That shit doesn't count. I say whatever to get the business. Fuck what you talking about."

The waitress came to the table and took our orders after placing two glasses of water in front of us. I ordered an eight ounce steak, loaded potato with extra cheese and bacon, broccoli, garlic bread, a salad with Italian dressing, and some fried asparagus. Justice ordered rib tips with fries and coleslaw.

"Your face looks good, boo. I'm glad you don't have any permanent scarring," Justice said, taking a sip of her water.

"Me too. I was scared I wouldn't be able to come back from the shit Tyson did to me. To be honest, he really spooked me with his antics. I'd never seen him like that before and I was shocked he took it that far. It's still a mystery as to why he did what he did. I mean, he was the one that wanted to end things with me."

"Tyson didn't expect the next man to come along as fast as Dap did. The saying goes, you don't miss what you had until it's gone. Plus, according to him, the grass wasn't greener on the other side and he thought he would have no problem easing back into your life."

"There's no way he would've thought some bullshit like that. Once it's over, that's it. Ain't no coming back. Especially when he thought he would find happiness in a bitch with not a hint of melanin in her skin. The way the world is set up today, that shit ain't happening too fuckin' often. It's too many low-key racist muthafuckas out there. Your president has fucked it up for everybody," I said, sipping my water.

The aroma of food floating around the restaurant had my stomach growling loudly. I glanced around, trying to see if the waitress was heading in our direction with our food. I did a double take when my eyes landed on the one muthafucka that we had talked up a few minutes prior. Tyson and his option were sitting enjoying themselves in the back corner close to the kitchen.

"Justice, Tyson is here," I said lowly.

"You lying," she said, about to turn around.

"Don't turn around. We're going to act like we don't see his ass."

That was short-lived because before I could lower my eyes, he caught sight of me and his smile turned into a frown the minute he spotted me. I immediately shot Dap a text and waited for him to respond. Our food arrived at that precise time and I concentrated on what was in front of me. As I cut into my steak, I could feel Tyson's glare from across the room, but I started a conversation with Justice while keeping my eyes on his ass.

"What is he doing?" Justice asked.

"Throwing daggers my way, but I'm not worried."

Faith took that opportunity to start fussing. Justice wiped her hands on the cloth napkin and reached into the diaper bag to prepare a bottle. My phone vibrated on the table and I grabbed it quickly because I knew it was Dap responding to the text I had sent him.

My love: Did that muthafucka say anything to you?

Me: No, but he keeps staring in my direction.

My love: I've been waiting on the day to get my hands on his ass. Continue to eat and he will be taken care of soon as he makes his way out of that bitch. You have nothing to worry about, Tana, I got this. Trust me, he's not stupid enough to try anything in a public place. Keep your cool.

Me: Okay. I'll see you soon.

My love: When you leave there, I told Juice to bring you to the store. I want to kiss your beautiful face and squeeze your ass LOL

Me: You're so silly. I'll be there soon as we finish eating.

We ate our food and Faith drifted off to sleep. Just as we were finishing our lunch, Tyson and his date walked past our table. He stopped and doubled back.

"Tana, I thought that was you," he smirked. "This is Rachel, my fiancée."

"Tyson, you know damn well I don't give a damn about who you're dating. Wait, is this the same Rachel whose parents didn't accept you because you're black? The one that you said you weren't fuckin' with anymore and wanted to make shit work with me? But when I turned you down, you broke in my home and raped, beat, and pissed on me? Get'cho ass outta my face with your stupid ass!"

"What is she talking about, Tyson?" Rachel asked, looking up at him.

"Baby, she's lying. Tana is the type of woman that don't do well with rejection and she's saying anything to have you upset with me. Including lying on me."

"Why would I lie on you when I have a man in my life and it's not you?" I said, smiling at him. "That shit pisses you off, doesn't it, Tyson?"

"Come on, baby. I'll see you around, Montana."

"Nah, you won't. Stay on the other side of the tracks, because you're no longer allowed over here anymore. Hey, Rach, talk to your man and tell him to stay the fuck away from me. Let me leave you with a tip, massage his shaft with your tongue as his dick glides down your throat. That gets him every time." I laughed.

Rachel's face turned beet red. She dropped his hand and stormed out of the door of the restaurant. I stared out the window as they got in Tyson's car and pulled off. A dark sedan with tinted windows pulled out behind them. I knew Dap had someone on Tyson's ass and he was going to be a distant memory by nightfall.

Meesha

Chapter 16

Dap

Customs was going strong and it was only two o'clock in the afternoon. There had been nonstop traffic and folks had been buying what I had in stock as well as custom jewelry. Twista, Common, and Chance the Rapper showed up to show love and ran fat checks as well. Chitown was showing up and showing out for me and I was loving every bit of it. My employees were taking care of business and I was right there in the mix with them to make shit shake.

I got the call from Tana and kind of fell out of my zone, but I bounced back without missing a beat. Business was flowing and all I heard was cha-ching every time I looked over at the long line of people. As I made my way toward the elevator, I stopped to admire the picture of Beverly and I. The smile on my face widened as I peeled my eyes away to push the button to head up to the second floor where the Customs apparel was located.

I stepped into the elevator when the doors opened. My phone vibrated and I removed it from the pockets of my slacks. There was a message from Tana informing me that nigga Tyson was at the restaurant she was went to. I immediately contacted Juice and told him about what was going on inside the restaurant. He wanted to go in and whoop his ass, but I had to let him know there was a time and place for everything.

After giving him strict instructions, I stepped off the elevator and walked into another crowd of people with Custom bags of clothing. The smile on my face was huge. I loved the sight before me and I was so glad I had made the decision to open up shop in Chicago.

"Donovan King, you outdid yourself with this place." A young woman stepped up to me smiling with a bag in her hand. "I was hoping I would see you to congratulate you in person," she said, placing her hand on my arm.

"Thank you," I replied as I took a step away from her. "Did you find anything you liked?"

"Actually, I did," she cheesed, batting her eyes. "I like you too." I couldn't catch the laugh that escaped my lips. "Did I say something funny?"

"No. Continue to shop, and thanks again for visiting Customs," I said, turning to walk away.

"How can I get to know you better, Mr. King?"

I stopped in my tracks. I didn't bother to turn around to address her. "There's no way for you to get to know me on a personal level, ma. I'm off the market and I'm in a happy space in my life. Enjoy the rest of your day."

"I mean, a man of your caliber can have more than one woman. I know how to play my position. What you got going on at home has nothing to do with me."

Turning to face her, I could feel the anger building up inside of me. This chick was used to dealing with fuck niggas and tried to run that shit on a real one. If I was even thinking about messing around on Tana, it sure as hell wouldn't have been with someone like her. Don't get me wrong, baby girl was fine as hell, but I knew for a fact that trouble was her middle name. Drama was pouring out of her pores like alcohol off a drunk. The way she licked her lips and gawked at me told me the only thing she saw was dollar signs. Nah, I wasn't falling for none of that.

"I'm a one woman man, love. Here's a little advice for you. Never lower your standards to win a nigga over. There's nothing cute about being number two when you can be number one in a man's life. Know your worth and don't settle for anything less than you deserve. You're beautiful and would be a good woman for someone. That someone just ain't me," I said calmly. "The next man you approach, make sure you display more than pussy. That shit doesn't work on authentic niggas like myself. Again, thank you for shopping at Customs. I appreciate you."

"Fuck yo' stuck up ass! I don't want none of this shit!" she said, throwing the bag full of items on a nearby display table and stalking toward the stairs.

I didn't give a damn if she didn't purchase anything. It only meant she was hanging around to get rejected and I made it happen.

Removing the clothing from the bag, I folded each item and placed them in their rightful places as some of the patrons glanced in my direction. Sharita, the manager of Customs, hurried in my direction as I straightened a pile of shirts.

"Is everything alright, Boss?" she asked.

"Yep. It was nothing I couldn't handle. Baby girl thought she was about to come up and I had to let her down easily. She didn't like that shit," I laughed.

"Oh, that's all? She'll be alright. I know exactly who she is. She's no longer allowed in the establishment. We don't need that type of negativity around here."

"Sharita, that's gon' happen more often than not. We want their money, so there's no use trying to keep them away. If they're buying, that's all I'm worried about. All that other bullshit is small to a giant. I know what I have at home so the task won't be hard to complete. The response will be the same for each and every one of them. I'm about to head upstairs to my office. If you need me, call my phone. Don't come up because I'm about to have a meeting."

"Okay, I have everything covered down here. See you tomorrow, Donovan." Sharita walked away to assist a customer and I went back to the elevator and punched the button for the third floor.

No one was allowed on the top floor of the building. At the grand opening, I had announced that Customs had music equipment. That was true, but the equipment wasn't the only thing on that level. The top level was my personal dungeon that was soundproofed with a small room for the equipment. The rest of the layout was an open space where I would teach niggas a lesson for fuckin' with what was mine, and that was exactly what was going to happen to Tyson when them Cali Boys brought his ass to see me.

***

The doorbell sounded and I looked at the monitor to see who was at the door. Kato and Judge were standing with a frightened Tyson standing between the two of them. I hit the button to release the lock. Judge entered first while Kato pushed Tyson forward with the butt of his gun. I sat back in the chair coolin' with a pool of smoke floating above my head. When Tyson laid eyes on me, he immediately started apologizing.

"I'm sorry, man. I didn't mean to say anything to Montana."

"Shut the fuck up!" My voice boomed as I stood to my feet rushing in his face. "How the hell are you a grown-ass man but didn't mean to say something? You sound like a real bitch right now. You're not here for opening yo' muthafuckin' mouth today, nigga! The shit you did a few weeks back is why yo' hoe ass is in front of me right now!"

"That was consensual—"

I drew my arm back and punched that nigga in his mouth. "Consensual my ass, muthafucka! You touched something that belongs to me and you won't live to do the shit to another female."

"Let me explain," he choked out with blood running out of his mouth.

"Go 'head. I wanna hear this shit," I said, folding my arms over my chest.

"Tana called me over to spend time with her. When I got there, she climbed in my lap and started kissing my neck. I asked if she was still fucking with you and she said no."

Every word out of his mouth was a lie and the only thing he was doing was pissing me off. Allowing him to continue telling his version of what happened, the only thing I could see was his mouth moving. I had tuned his ass all the way out. My arms dropped from my chest and went to the small of my back. When my hand gripped the handle of my Glock .38, I pulled it and shot Tyson between his muthafuckin' eyes.

His body fell and his head hit the pavement with a thud. I saw nothing but red as I watched his bodily fluids escape through his pants. Tyson's eyes were wide open, but there was no life left in them.

"Dump his ass in the tub of acid in that back room," I said, heading to the bathroom on the other side of the room.

Changing out of the tailored suit I had worn to the store, I pulled on an all-black Customs T-shirt and a pair of black jeans. Stepping into my black and white Balenciaga sneakers, I pulled a black fitted onto my head, turned the light off, and walked back to my office to answer my ringing phone.

"Yeah, baby."

"I'm downstairs on the first floor. Where are you?" Tana asked.

"I'll be right there. Give me a few minutes." Ending the call, I made my way to the back room and Kato and Judge were walking toward me. "Is that nigga a distant memory?"

"No trace of his ass, not even a tooth particle." Judge smiled.

"Damn, Dap. I forgot how the fuck you got down, nigga! You still got it."

"You can take the nigga out the streets, but you can't take the streets out the nigga. Remember that, Kato. Muthafuckas gon' stop lettin' a muthafuckin' suit fool they ass. I'm still the same mutha-fucka; my pockets just a lil fatter. I gotta go, my baby's downstairs." I snatched my leather Customs jacket off the back of the door and zipped it up.

"We need to talk about Lucci and Arturro. They checked out of the hotel the other day. We haven't been able to track them. They're up to something, Dap," Judge said as we walked to the back door.

"They are next on the list. Tell Christian I'll be through later this evening," I replied, letting them leave. I followed suit locking up.

Judge and Kato jumped in the rental that was parked behind the store and peeled out as I walked around to the front of the store. Spotting the SUV that Juice was driving, I peeked inside and his ass wasn't in it. He had to be inside with Tana and Justice; at least that's where his ass better had been. Reaching out to grasp the handle to go inside Customs, a hand landed on my forearm and I laid eyes on Kalene through the glass.

"I just need to talk to you, Donovan. Why are you making this so hard for me?" she asked.

Shrugging her hand off me, I turned around and pushed her back a few feet. The last thing I needed was for Tana to see Kalene all up on me. It was chilly as fuck in the Chi, but her ass had on a mini dress with thigh high boots and a little-ass leather jacket like it was summer time.

"Like I said at the club Friday, there's nothing to discuss. You made your decision when you left me in Cali."

"Do you even want to know why I left?"

"No, it doesn't matter. In my mind, my money wasn't long enough for you so, you bounced. That's cool, Kalene." I hunched my shoulders.

"That's far from the truth and you know it. I have my own money, Donovan."

"Kalene, I haven't seen your name in the spotlight in a minute. You're not even modeling anymore, so save that shit for somebody else. Your well is dry and you're back trying to get on this money train you heard and read about. It's too late. There's already a First Lady of Customs, and it's not you. I had that spot reserved for you for many years, but you didn't even have the decency to reach out to a nigga. You snooze, you lose, ma."

"You will never love anyone the way you loved me, Dap." Kalene smirked, wiping at her nose.

"You're right. I love her ten times more than I've ever loved you. She's going to be Mrs. Donovan King real soon. As a matter of fact, I have to go. My future wife is waiting for me inside."

I turned to go into the building and Kalene grabbed me by my arm. I glanced down at her hand. She removed her hand and stared me in the eyes. I waited for her to say what she had to say but instead, she started scratching her neck and rubbing her nose vigorously. My eyebrows furrowed as I watched her closely.

"Kalene, you on that shit?" I asked, dropping my hand from the door handle.

"Hell nawl! I would never do drugs. It's not good for the profession I'm in."

"And what profession is that? An extra in the remake of *New Jack City*? You trying to get the role as the prom fiend?" I smirked. "That's a junkie itch if I've ever seen one," I said looking her up and down stopping at her thighs. There were track marks in the inner part of her legs.

"What the fuck ever, Dap," she said putting her hands in the pockets of her jacket. "I want to start over. Can we at least talk about that?"

"Nope," I stated without hesitation. "Anything else? It seems like you made a blank trip to Chicago when all you had to do was make a phone call. This could've been handled within a few minutes and you would've still had all the money spent to do whatever you do with your money."

The door to Customs opened and Tana stepped out with a scowl on her face. Knowing it was a matter of time before she would make her exit, I was glad she chose to show her face because obviously, Kalene thought I was lying about having a woman.

"How long does it take to tell a muthafucka to get out your face, Dap?" Tana asked, letting her coat fall open.

"Tana, what did I tell you about calling me that shit? I was trying to get in but as you can see, I've been stuck out here talking about a bunch of nothing."

"Aw, that's cute. I remember when you used to get mad when I called you Dap as well." Kalene chuckled. The way Tana's head shot in Kalene's direction, I knew shit was not about to go well for her. She should've left when she had the chance.

"Hey, I'm Tana, and you are?"

"Oh, I'm Kalene, his ex," she smiled with her hand held out. Tana looked down at her outstretched hand and brought her eyes back to Kalene's face.

"That means you're an ex for a reason, right? See, I heard all about how you acted at the club last week. Let's get something straight, Kalene. If I know Donovan the way I believe I know him, he has told you one too many times there's nothing to discuss between the two of you."

"This is between Donovan and myself. It has nothing to do with you at all!" Kalene shouted.

"That's where you're wrong. We are one, sweetie, and don't nothing shake without consultation with me. So whatever you are trying to accomplish has everything to do with me."

Kalene's eyes traveled to the Custom charm that hung from Tana's neck and the expression on her face was priceless. When we were together, I sat up late one night and designed the charm with Kalene by my side. Never thinking much about it after she left, I went back and made some alterations when Tana captured a nigga's heart turning the creation into the masterpiece that hung around my baby's neck.

"That's how you're doing shit now, Donovan? I helped you come up with the concept for that charm!" Kalene snapped.

"That's not the same design we came up with. Stop with the extra shit, Kalene. Look, it's cold as hell out here and like I've told you before, there's nothing more to discuss. It's done between us. There will be no coming back. Ever."

"It's because of this bitch!" she snarled.

Kalene lunged at Tana and my hand wrapped around her neck in a quick motion. "If you even think about putting your hands, on her I'll kill yo' monkey ass in broad daylight," I said, cutting off her air supply for a second before pushing her away.

"You didn't have to stop her, babe. That bitch would've swung and needed assistance getting to her car. Your best bet will be to get on the next thing smoking and get as far away from Chicago as possible. This is one tree you don't want to bark around." Tana stood her ground and didn't flinch when Kalene came at her. There was no way I was about to let her fight a bitter bitch over something I made perfectly clear.

"Nah, you don't need to be fighting. You are about to be the mother of my child and I need the two of you safe," I said, pecking Tana on the lips.

"A baby? Really, Donovan?"

"Don't be surprised, Kalene. We weren't meant to be. Go back where you came from and stay away from my establishment. Being on stupid shit is not going to get you what you're seeking, so don't even try it. You would only put yourself in the line of fire to come up missing. Good day."

I opened the door to Customs and guided Tana inside before I followed close behind. Kalene was left on the outside looking in with defeat written on her face. She wasn't going to be on the shit like Shanell so I wasn't worried about any type of retaliation from her. If didn't nobody know about Dap, Kalene surely did. She didn't want any of the backlash that came with crossing me.

Meesha

Chapter 17

Shanell

I sat watching the interaction between Dap and the bitch I overheard talking to the Italians at his event and I laughed. All the King's men must have had that golden-tipped dick to have all the ladies going crazy over their asses. Whatever the bitch said pissed him off bad enough for him to yoke her ass up. The funniest part was how he left her goofy ass standing there looking like a wounded puppy. It couldn't have been me because I would've tore all that shit up, right along with his muthafuckin' ass.

"That shit was wild, wasn't it?"

Looking up from my seat in front of Jamba Juice, one of the Italian guys that I was just thinking about walked over from the street. I was confused as to why he was even talking to me like I was familiar with him. Instead of responding, I looked back in the direction of Dap's store and the woman was nowhere in sight.

"Mind if I have a seat?" he asked. He pulled out the chair anyway without waiting for a reply and I stood to leave. "You don't have to leave, beautiful. I noticed you sitting here and recognized you from the club the other night. I'm Luciano, but everyone calls me Lucci."

He extended his hand and I grabbed it as I eased back into the seat. "Nice to meet you. I remember you from that night. Ole girl that was talking to Dap was there with you. Why didn't you go to her defense when he choked the fuck outta her?" I laughed.

"She was on her own with that shit. I tried to talk her out of going over there to talk to his ass. He doesn't want her anymore. So, you know Donovan?"

"Yeah, I know his ass. What's your affiliation with him? You seem to know him as well."

"I know him from back in California. He's an alright guy."

"Stop lying, nigga. I know there's some bitter blood between y'all from the little bit I heard sitting at the bar at the club. You don't have to attempt picking my brain to see where I stand with his ass. Just so you know, I don't fuck with him at all."

"I figured that much when you hauled ass that night when they came down the stairs. What did you do to make them chase you down like a criminal?" Lucci asked.

"Why do you want to know? I don't know nothing about you but you're trying to be all in my business." I scowled.

"Slow down, baby. The attitude isn't needed right now. I peeped the animosity you have with them, that's all. Maybe we can help one another because I have beef with that muthafucka too. Dap has something that belongs to me and I want it. Kalene, the woman you saw him talking to was supposed to get close to him for me, but the bitch is still in her feelings. He won't give her ass the time of day and I need to go another route."

Sitting back in the chair, I listened to him pour out his faulty plan and I was rather intrigued knowing I might have back up with getting revenge on the King family. When I went back to the hotel after getting away from Wes and his brother, Sage little ass was no-where to be found. I knew his ass had called somebody to rescue him. It let me know Wes had a search party looking for me and I had to be very careful about where I showed up in the city.

Hiding in the city where I lived was beginning to be a task, but I'd learned how to be inconspicuous whenever I wanted to be close to one of them muthafuckas. Killing Beverly gave me an orgasm I wouldn't get again until I sent somebody else to meet their maker. The feeling would come sooner rather than later and I couldn't wait.

I stared Lucci straight in the eyes. "What made you comfortable enough to approach me in this manner? I mean, you don't know shit about me but you want me to help you in a drastic situation. Make this shit make sense to me," I said seriously.

"I don't want to stay this close to my target. Would you mind coming to my hotel so we can talk about this in private? The last thing I need is Dap seeing us together down the street from his place of business. I swear I'm only trying to talk, nothing more."

"What makes you think I want to go to your hotel room? We can go to another location, but your hotel is not going to work for me. I don't know shit about you and one thing I don't do is trust anyone's word. Dap and his brother are out for blood when it comes to me, I don't know who's on their team to get at me. You could be on their team to kill my black ass."

"I swear, I'm not working with them. My father left Dap a lot of shit when he was killed and his ass don't deserve any of it. He had two sons and left us the bare minimum, but I know with my father being a billionaire, he left the bulk of his assets to that nigger!"

"You got me fucked up, Lucci, or whatever your name is. I'm black as hell and you won't sit here disrespecting my race. I don't give a damn what you are allowed to do back in California, but you won't address my people as niggas in my presence. Is that clear?"

A gleam of fire was present in his eyes, but he shook that shit off because Lucci knew deep down, he had to respect what the fuck I said, especially if he wanted my help in getting his money from Dap. A billionaire? Shid, hearing that made me want to come on to Dap's ass and suck his dick to get close to his pockets myself. No wonder the Kalene bitch was trying to get in good with Dap. That was a sweet come up.

"I have no respect for Dap and he will always be a nigger to me. If I offended you in anyway, I apologize," Lucci said, standing to his feet. "Would you mind accompanying me to my hotel? The proposition I have in store for you will be one you wouldn't want to pass up. There's a hefty price tag on it that will be worth every penny."

When he threw monetary value in the mix, I knew I was all in. The money was a small part of why I was considering hearing him out, but that print in the front of his pants was what really had my attention. For a white boy, his ass was packing something serious and my inner self was ready to fuck. She was getting her seduction antics prepared as I licked my lips thinking about all the nasty shit I wanted to do with his pale ass.

"Your apology is accepted, but I want you to know that a nigger is an ignorant muthafucka. Anybody can be one, not just a black person. Don't say that shit around me no more. Let's go before you piss me off more than you have. Where are you staying?" I asked, rising from the chair I was sitting in.

"I'm staying at the Whitehall Hotel on the Magnificent Mile."

"You sound like a fuckin' tourist," I laughed. "I know exactly where you're staying. I'll meet you there. Just stand outside and wait for me," I said, sashaying down the street to my car.

As I walked, I could feel someone watching me and assumed it was Lucci. When I turned my head to look over my shoulder, he was nowhere in sight, but the eerie feeling of being watched was still strong around me. Hitting the key fob for the rental, I pulled the handle and opened the door. A car pulled alongside me as I was getting inside. A dark-skinned guy with locs and what looked like a diamond grill in his mouth leaned out of the passenger window with a smirk on his face.

"You may want to stay away from Lucci. His ass will be dead soon and you're too damn sexy to be affiliated with him anyway. What's a sista like yourself doing entertaining white meat? He must've offered you a large amount of money, huh?"

"I don't even know him. He came up to me and for your information, I don't discriminate when it comes to people. I love everyone, to be honest," I responded in my proper voice. If they knew Lucci, that only meant they were on Dap's team.

Getting inside the rental, I closed the door and started the ignition quickly. The car was still parked next to me and there was no way for me to pull out of the park until they moved. My heart was thumping in my chest because I didn't know if they knew who I was or not. The thought of getting shot was the only thing on my mind and there was nothing I could do to prevent it. Dude waved his hand to get my attention, causing me to roll the window down a little bit.

"Would you move so I can be on my way?" I asked nicely.

"I have a question. Did Lucci say where he was staying?"

"Why would he tell me where he's staying? I don't even know him to be worried about his living situation. All I know is he's not from here by his accent. I can say the same about you too." I smirked.

"You're right. I'm not from here. I'm Cali bred and these muthafuckas from Chicago ain't got shit on us. What are you on later, shawty?"

"I'm not on nothing. I won't be giving you my number or any of that type of shit, so don't ask. I'm on my way to meet my man and have a nice time with him."

"Aight, well let me get out of your hair and let yo' stuck up ass go meet your lame ass nigga. Remember, stay away from Lucci."

The car sped down the street and I waited a few minutes before I pulled onto the street, heading to the hotel where Lucci was staying. It took about five minutes for me to park in front of the hotel and Lucci was standing outside as I requested. The valet attendant walked to my driver's door and pulled it open after Lucci greased his palm.

"Welcome to the Whitehall Hotel," he said smiling.

Nodding my head, I exited the vehicle and placed my hand in Lucci's outstretched one. I hope you're hungry. I took the liberty of ordering something to eat while we talked business," he explained as we entered the hotel.

"A girl is always down to eat," I replied.

We entered the elevator that opened the minute we walked up and Lucci pressed the button for the fifteenth floor. The only sound that was heard was the soft dings as the elevator rose upward. When it stopped, an automated voice announced that we had arrived on the designated floor. Lucci motioned for me to exit first and touched the small of my back. The gesture sent a shiver up my spine.

I stepped into the room. There was a living room straight ahead and I went to the sofa and took a seat. Lucci took off his jacket and laid it across the back of the sofa and sat down on the loveseat in front of me. He hiked his pants up before he sat down. All I saw was dick and my mouth began to water profusely.

"Do you have any water in here?" I asked, glancing around the room.

"Yes," he said reaching into the mini fridge. "What is your relationship with Dap?" he asked, handing me the bottled water.

"I don't have a relationship with Dap. His problem with me is based on his punk-ass brother."

"What's your problem with his brother then?"

"I killed his muthafuckin' mama! I thought we were here to talk about how you're going to get your shit back from Dap. You're asking the wrong shit."

"Oh shit! You're the one that laid his old lady down. We are one and the same, I killed my old man since he wanted to ration out his money. I'm waiting for the lawyer to get back with me about his will. My brother and I was the beneficiary on that shit."

I looked at him like he was crazy before I went in on his ass. "You killed your father for insurance money? What type of shit you and your brother on? That's shit only white muthafuckas do. Were y'all trying to be in the headlines like the Menendez brothers or some shit?"

"It's not a white thing at all, so don't try to make this about race. I'm not white either. I'm Italian; get it right. Black people kill their parents sometimes too."

"Not for money," I laughed. "If a black muthafucka kills their parents, it's going to be for a reason. Abuse, molestation, neglect, you know, something drastic. Money is never a reason for someone black to kill their daddy."

"Whatever. I introduced myself when we met, but you have yet to give me your name," Lucci said changing the subject.

"You can call me Shan. Let me ask you a question. Why kill your father if he was a billionaire?"

"Like I said, he only gave us what he wanted to give. That shit wasn't enough for me."

"So you're basically saying you fucked off your money and expected your father to constantly dish out his hard-earned cash whenever you wanted?"

"Why not? He has done it my whole life but wanted me to work for money he gave me freely for years."

"It never crossed your mind to put money to the side for a rainy day? I'm just trying to understand all of this. Don't get upset about my line of questioning."

"Why would I save when my father has money hand over fist? That doesn't make sense at all. I could've invested in something productive but, for what? My father was loaded."

I chuckled before taking a sip of water. "That privilege shit is a muthafucka, I see. What is it that Dap has that belongs to you, if you don't mind me asking?"

"Customs. That was a business my father just handed over to that ni—punk. My father built that company and it belongs to my brother and I."

Lucci sounded like a spoiled-ass brat, but more like a bitch if you asked me. I didn't agree with the reason he killed his father and I was guilty of killing my mama, but the shit wasn't for something as stupid as this dude. At least his father was there for his greedy ass. Let me find out what the fuck he had in mind for getting back at Dap.

"Tell me, what is your plan?" I asked, leaning back on the plush sofa.

"I don't have one because the only place I know to locate him is the store. With you on my team, maybe I can get more inside information on him."

"Dap is not my target, as I've told you before. I know where his brother and father lives. Other than that, I don't know much about Dap other than he moved back here from California and opened Customs. He was only added to my list because he put his nose in my business with his brother. Get ready to run to the car and cry because Customs is going to get burned to the ground tonight."

I took another sip of water and waited for Lucci to voice his thoughts on my plan. When he just sat without responding, I continued. "The entire family will be burying Beverly soon. The problem with catching them there is, I no longer have an inside connect on what's happening in their lives. Oh, they are on your ass too."

"What do you mean?" Lucci asked.

"When I got in my car to come here, a couple of Cali dudes pulled up on me and told me to stay away from you because you would be dying soon. I let them believe I was a random female that you were trying to come on to. Your location is safe; for now."

My phone rang and I dug around in my purse to find it. Glancing at the screen, I saw it was a call coming in from Wes. Answering it was out of the question. They had Sage so I knew he was really trying to track me down. Talking to him was not in my plans especially since I knew he wanted me dead. Finding a way to get at him first was my main concern.

There was a knock on the door and Lucci got up to answer it. When he returned, he was pushing a cart to the table sitting on the other side of the room. I watched as he unloaded dish after dish and my stomach growled. The lobster tails, crab legs, potatoes, asparagus, and other food items sent off an aroma that I couldn't ignore. I was ready to pig out and hop on that Italian dick to see if he knew how to work that monster I saw through his pants.

Chapter 18

Justice

Wes had to go into the office and that was the reason I went out with Tana. Seeing Tyson at the restaurant pissed me off because I wanted to beat his ass. Luck was on his side because I had my baby with me. When Juice took me and Faith back to the house, I fed her before giving her a bath. Baby girl was tired as hell and fell out like she had worked a full eight-hour shift. Turning the monitor on before leaving the nursery, I went straight to my bedroom and took a quick shower.

Exiting the bathroom wrapped in a plush towel, I turned the Bluetooth speaker on and connected my phone. I was sleepy, but I wanted to drift off to sleep to some old school R&B tunes. The first song that came on was Sade's *Ordinary Love* and he sultry voice flowed from the speakers. Grooving over to the king-sized bed I shared with my husband, I pulled the covers back, dropped the towel in the hamper, and placed my phone on the nightstand before climbing into the bed.

My mind went back to the chick that had popped up on Wes at Customs. Her presence didn't sit well with me and I couldn't figure out why she would travel all the way to Chicago to try and win Dap over. She had left him a year ago then suddenly popped back up out of the blue? Nah, something wasn't right with that at all.

I was proud of the way Tana handled the situation though. She didn't get mad at her man and just let the bitch know there was a new sheriff in town for the man she left dry. Pregnancy has calmed her down a bit because the old Tana would've beat that girl's ass. Tana's words alone left that woman looking like she wanted to break down and cry.

Driftin' on a memory
Ain't no place I'd rather be
Than with you, yeah
Lovin' you, well, well, well
Day will make a way for night

All we need is candlelight
and a song, yeah
Soft and long, well

My parents used to step to this song every Friday night and it was one of my favorites. It showed me how love was supposed to be early on. Wes and I had our problems these last couple months, but our love was strong enough to endure anything. Letting someone come between what we had wasn't going to happen.

I hated the fact that Beverly lost her life behind the bullshit and I wasn't looking forward to saying goodbye to the sweetest person I'd ever met outside of my own mother. Since the night of her passing, Wes hadn't really showed much emotion but I knew it was coming. Getting myself prepared for his breakdown was something I was working on perfecting.

The soulful music played lowly, relaxing my body so much that it put me in a semi-coma. The foot of the bed dipped at my feet, but I couldn't pry my eyes open for anything in the world. Soft kisses were planted along the inside of my legs and at first, I thought I was dreaming. Wes and I hadn't been very intimate as of late.

My love bud grew the closer the kisses got to my lower region. My fantasy became a reality as his fingers separated my thick lips and his tongue glided from the bottom of my kitty to the top. The shiver that quaked my spine was electric. Arching my back from the bed, I grabbed the back of his head and pushed it forward so he could devour my goodies.

I moaned lowly as I grinded my hips. "Shit, right there, baby." The dam broke immediately and the river flowed through the levee. My husband's tongue cleaned up the mess it made as my body continued to quake. Climbing onto the bed, Wes positioned himself between my legs and pried them open with his knees. Gliding his tool along my love box, he eased my best friend in and slowly stroked as he kissed me deeply.

"I love you so much, Mrs. King," Wes whispered in my ear as he caressed my silky walls.

"I love you too, baby," I moaned.

We made love for hours and then fell asleep in one another's arms. The sound of Wes' phone jolted him awake and my eyes automatically went to the digital clock on the dresser. It was one in the morning and the first thing that came to mind was that something had happened.

"What's up, brah?" Wes asked into the phone. He was silent for a few seconds before he jumped up and turned on the light. "I'm on my way," he said, scrambling around the room throwing on clothes.

"What's going on, bae?" I asked, sitting up in the bed.

"That was Dap. Customs is on fire and he is going ballistic. When the fuck is shit gon' stop happening around this muthafucka? It's like there's a dark cloud hanging over our heads and we can't seem to get away from it." Wes sat on the end of the bed and tied his shoes before grabbing his keys and wallet from the dresser.

"Babe, I think you should take a quick shower first."

"I'll be back. This is the best fragrance around. Niggas is going to want to purchase this shit," he smirked. "For real, I don't have time for all of that. My brother needs me," he replied, walking to my side of the bed and kissing me deeply. "I love you, Jus. I'll keep you posted, but this shit got Shanell written all over it."

"Be careful, babe, I love you too."

Snuggling under the covers, I tried my best to go back to sleep, but it was a hard task to accomplish. Faith started whining and it was my cue to get up to check on my princess. As I entered the nursery, Faith starting wailing at the top of her lungs soon as I walked in.

"Hey, mama. You're doing the most right now. What's the problem, Faye?" I asked, lifting her out of the crib. "Ohhh, you stinky."

Placing her onto the changing table, I removed her sleeper and tossed it into the hamper. I gathered everything I would need to make Faith smell like a baby again. Once Faith was cleaned up, I put her in the crib while I made a bottle for her.

"Okay, baby. Let's go chill in my room," I said, making my way out of the nursery.

I laid Faith in the bassinet on the other side of the room while I changed the sheets on my bed. There was no way I could have my child lying on all of her daddy kids that didn't make it. I took the opportunity to hop in the shower quickly after making the bed, I cradled Faith in my arms, burped her, and she went back to sleep like the fat kid she was.

Chirp, chirp.

The sound of the door opening downstairs caught my attention and I sprang out of the bed. Wes hadn't been gone a full thirty minutes and I knew for a fact it took twenty to get downtown in traffic. There was no way he would be back so soon.

Movement could be heard coming from somewhere on the main floor of the house and I automatically grabbed my daughter and headed for the closet. Pushing the button on the hidden panel on the wall, I crawled into the safe room that Wes insisted we needed and hit the speaker to hear what was going on in the house.

"There's no one here. The house is too quiet," a male's voice said in a low tone.

"The bitch is here. We watched Dap's brother leave and no one was with him. They have a baby, right? They're in this muthafucka. We going upstairs because nothing is going on down here."

The safe room was soundproof so if Faith cried, they wouldn't hear her. Standing to my feet, I went deeper into the room and grabbed Wes' nine-millimeter and checked the clip. Whoever the hell thought it was alright to come into my home was going to wish they hadn't. Moving Faith away from the door I sat Indian style on the floor and continued to listen quietly.

"The nursery is empty. Did you find anything in here?"

"No. She's here somewhere." The voice was coming closer to the safe door and I could hear hangers being moved around. It was going to be a matter of time before the safe room button would be found. I didn't hit the lock purposely because I had something hot for both of them niggas.

"Oh, yeah. She's behind this wall."

When I heard the button being pushed, I cocked the gun and stood to my feet. As the door slowly opened, I pulled the trigger three times, hitting the first dude in the middle of his chest. Watching his body fall to the carpeted floor, I raised my eyes and the second dude let of a round hitting me in my left arm.

"Fuck!" I cringed, moving into the darkness. Faith took that moment to start crying from the loud gunshot sound. Blood was seeping through the nightshirt I had on and my entire arm was numb.

"You're not going to make it out of here alive, bitch! You might as well show your face."

"Bring your bad ass in and get me, pussy! Do I look stupid enough come out so you can shoot me like I did your homie? It won't be that easy to take me from my child."

"Hold on, Caesar, I'm going to get you to the hospital."

I could hear the dude that shot me trying to get his homie out of the closet. I took that opportunity to show my face. The idiot thought I was going to hide until they were gone? Nah, that's not how I play. With all the strength I could muster, I raised my left arm and steadied the gun with the right. Stepping into plain sight, the muthafucka underestimated me like I thought and had all of his attention on the wrong shit.

While he was trying to get a grip on his partner, I let off one shot in the top of his head. Blood splattered on both sides of the closet, covering all articles of clothing in its path. His body fell on top of the already wounded guy. I knew he was dead so I pushed his body to the side and stood over the dude that was struggling to breathe with a hole in his chest.

"Who the fuck sent you?" I asked with the nine pointed in his face.

"Fuck. You. Bitch!"

"I swear, if you tell me what I want to know, I will call an ambulance for you."

"It's against the code. I'm not telling you shit!"

"That's cool. I'll see you in hell, muthafucka," I gritted before emptying the clip into his body.

I went through his pockets. He had a stack of money and a cell phone on him. The gun that he had was resting on top of my favorite pair of Giuseppe stilettos. The iPhone 11Max was locked. I raised the phone to the punk's face, but the phone didn't unlock. Holding his eyes open with my thumb and forefinger, I tried again and it worked.

I went right to the text messages and I found out everything I needed to know. Walking back into the safe room, I picked up my daughter and stepped over both bodies before exiting the closet and closing the door. After placing Faith in her bassinet, I went into the settings of the phone and changed the settings on the phone to change the code so I'd be able to get back in it.

Once I had Faith settled, I placed the gun on the nightstand and picked up my phone to call Wes. As I listened to the phone ring, I got frustrated because his phone went to voicemail. Ending the call, I pressed his name again and listened as the phone rang.

"Yeah, bae? Sorry for not answering, it's hectic as hell down here. I'm fine and I'll see you when I get home. These bitch ass police are on extra shit and I have to get off this phone."

"Before you hang up, we have some bullshit of our own here at the house. There are two sacks of *California* potatoes in the closet. I need you to throw them out expeditiously," I said talking in code. "I left them there until you get home and you should get here soon as possible."

"California potatoes? What the hell are you talking about, Justice?"

"How the hell can I put this so you can understand? Umm, I have two stray dogs from California trapped in our bedroom closet and they need to go to the pound."

"You're talking in circles and I told you I have to deal with these damn cops. I'll see you when I get home, okay?"

Wes ended the call and it pissed me off. I'd been out of the game so long I couldn't think of any of the lingo we used back in the day. I irritated the fuck out of myself so I knew he was still trying to figure out what I was talking about.

I tried my luck with Donovan. His phone went straight to voicemail and I didn't want to call him back. Instead, I called Wes Sr. and told him to tell Spencer to come to the house with him. There was no way I was staying in the house with two dead bodies. Somebody had to get these muthafuckas out quickly.

Meesha

Chapter 19

Wes

When I turned the corner onto Michigan Avenue, I had to park down the street because it seemed like the entire Chicago Fire Department was trying to fight the flames coming out of Customs and a few stores on both sides of the building. I saw the flames and smoke as I was driving toward the store, but I didn't think it was bad as it actually was. There wasn't going to be shit left to salvage. Dap worked hard getting that store up and running and it was destroyed in less than a week's time.

I was stopped the moment I tried to get close to my brother as the police surrounded him as if he was a suspect. Detective Roman and his partner Detective Barnett was the two muthafuckas that stood out to me amongst all the uniformed cops. They hadn't been around since accusing Dap and I of murkin' that nigga Curt.

"Why would I burn down my own fuckin' store?" I heard my brother ask, staring daggers at Detective Roman. "I put blood, sweat, and tears into getting my shit up and running and you think I did this shit? Get the fuck outta my face with that bullshit, you sound stupid as fuck!" I heard Dap shout out loud.

"Look, that's my brother over there and I'm just trying to make sure he's alright," I said to the officer that was trying to play security.

"Ay, Roman!"

Detective Roman turned in the direction his name was called. He laid eyes on me and smirked before giving a signal to let me through. Before I could get to Dap, my phone rang and I let it go to voicemail. When it rang again and I pulled it from my pocket, I saw it was Justice calling. She was talking crazy and I told her I would see her when I got home. Walking up to my brother, he was fuming.

"Just the person I needed to see. Do you know who could've set your brother's establishment afire?" Detective Roman asked.

"Nah, but it seems you're accusing my brother of this shit. He didn't have anything to do with any of this," I stated, crossing my arms over my chest and parting my legs.

"Just like the two of you had nothing to do with Curtis Miles's death, huh?" he smirked.

"We already told you how you could clear us of that bullshit. You can come better than that. The reason you are here this morning is because my brother's business is burning to smithereens before our eyes. Did you check the surveillance cameras we told you about? If not, do your fuckin' job!"

"This is no coincidence, Mr. King. Wasn't your mother murdered recently? I guess that had nothing to do with you either, huh?" Detective Roman's snide remark almost got his shit rocked.

"What the fuck does my mother's death have to do with anything? You're trying to compare apples and oranges and that shit won't work with me. That's law enforcement's job to find out as well as who the fuck set fire to my brother's shit!"

"Let me ask you this, Mr. King. Did you all find the missing kid that was supposed to be home with your mother when she was attacked?"

I didn't know where his line of questioning was going but he was treading on thin ice interrogating me about some shit he wasn't even involved in. "Yeah, Sage was dropped off on my father's doorstep a couple days after my mother's death. We don't know who had him and neither does he. We questioned him and he couldn't tell us who snatched him up."

"So you're going to stand in my face and lie, Mr. King? According to the police statement, your mother's neighbor said a Shanell Jones was the one that took the boy."

"His muthafuckin' name is Sage! He didn't mention anything about Shanell when he was returned to my father!" I seethed.

"Well, we're going to have to talk with him. I want to hear his version of what happened."

"One thing you won't be doing is interrogating my son! How about we talk about this shit right here?" I said, pointing behind me at Customs. "This is the reason you're here, right? Keep your ass on task before you piss me off. Leave my son and my mother out of your bullshit, Roman. Don't make me repeat myself."

"I'll keep that in mind, but this is far from over. You are looking at twenty-five to life for the murder of Curtis Miles," he said sizing me up. "I have the perfect outfit for you to wear, son." Detective Roman laughed.

"You're barking up the wrong tree. That's one murder you won't pin on me or my brother. We will be in your office real soon with our lawyer. Your threats may work for these niggas that don't know any better, but that shit would never work on me. Now get the fuck away from me."

Detective Roman turned to Dap and crossed his arms. "Are you insured?" he asked calmly.

"Of course, I am. What type of question is that?" Dap through back at him.

"I mean, I've seen things like this happen with many business owners that are hard up for money. They would open an establishment, then destroy it for insurance money. You could be one of the same."

Dap laughed and shook his head at Detective Roman. "See, I bet the business owners you are referring to are white muthafuckas. See, I'm a black nigga that ain't been in need of money for a very long time. I've worked hard for everything I have and I wouldn't jeopardize my business or reputation for a dollar. I started Customs when I was a teenager and got it where it is on my own." Dap snapped.

"If you did your homework before you stepped to me talking stupid, you would know that Donovan King is a self-made billionaire. Just because I'm not out here being flashy doesn't mean I'm broke and looking for a come up. The problem may well be that you're trying to figure out how I'm making more money than you make in a year."

Detective Roman's face turned beet red after hearing Dap's words. The only thing he could do was look at my brother because whatever he thought to say, couldn't pass his lips. I knew first hand that Dap would've had a clean comeback for his ass if he did find his voice.

"I'll be in touch with both of you. Have a nice night and stay out of trouble. I have my eye on you boys. Come on, Barnett, let's get out of here."

"Yeah, do that. And for the record, keep harassing me and my brother and the city of Chicago are going to add to my bankroll. We didn't kill Curt. While you're so adamant about pinning this shit on us, you could be trying to find the real killer," Dap shot out as the two detectives walked away.

The fire chief walked up to Dap and let him know that the building had been declared condemned and he would have to contact his insurance company and file a claim. There was going to be a full investigation conducted and they would keep Dap posted on their findings. We were given the okay to leave when my phone rang. Pulling it out of my pocket, I saw it was Pops calling and it was well past two in the morning.

"Hey, Pops. Is everything alright with Sage?" I asked as soon as the call connected.

"Sage is at Donovan's house. You need to get yo' ass home now!" he said sternly into the phone.

"What's going on?" I asked, waving for Dap to follow me.

"I can't explain over the phone, but Justice said she called and told you to come home! Where the fuck is you anyway?" he snapped.

"Downtown. Customs was burned to the ground and Dap called and I came to his aid. What the fuck is so important that you're scolding me like I'm a kid?"

"Just get yo' ass to your place of residence now! You got fifteen minutes, and bring your brother with you."

My father hung up on me and I was puzzled. First Justice called talking in riddles, now my pops said the bare minimum and I was still in the dark. Shit just didn't make sense to me.

"Brah, what's going on?" Dap asked.

"I don't know, but follow me to the crib. Something is wrong, but neither Pops nor Justice is saying what it is over the phone. We have to go see what's up for ourselves. I'll see you there," I said, running across the street to my whip.

***

When I pulled up to my crib, I spotted Pops' car as well as uncle Spence's. I jumped out and Dap was right on my ass. Soon as we entered the house, Pops was in my face in a flash.

"What the fuck is going on, Wes?" His voice bounced off the walls of the foyer.

"Customs was burned down—"

"I'm not talking about Customs! Go upstairs and look in the closet in your bedroom!"

I stood looking at him because he was coming at me about some shit I had no knowledge of. Justice stepped into the foyer with Faith in her arms. The grim look on her face let me know something terrible happened while I was gone.

"Go upstairs and see what the fuck is going on! She will explain what happened after the fact. You're wasting time standing there looking stupid as fuck."

The only time Pops talked like that was when one of us had messed up tremendously. I made my way to the stairs and climbed them slowly. Dap was right behind me as usual and it had been that way since we were younger. He never let me get in a world of trouble alone. We were always side by side every step of the way.

"Nigga, open the door!" Dap screamed as I stood in front of the closet without moving.

Doing as instructed, I yanked the door open and two white muthafuckas were lying on the closet floor turning purple. Both of them were dead as fuck, but the only thing on my mind was, what the hell were they doing in my shit?

"Who the fuck are these niggas?" I asked out loud. Dap walked around me and peered inside the closet. After taking a closer look, he walked further inside and kneeled in front of the bodies.

"This is Piero. He is one of Lucci's henchmen. This muthafucka is Franco," he said, pointing to the one with the hole in the top of his head. "Lucci sent these niggas in yo' shit to get back at me. Why you were targeted is something I can't figure out at this point. I'm so sorry my shit has landed at your doorstep, brah."

It's not your fault, Dap. The same way you were riding with me to get at Shanell, I'm rockin' with you to get at these muthafuckas," I said, watching Dap go through the pockets of each body.

"I'm taking this money and putting it in my niece's bank. What are they going to do with it? Not a damn thing. Where the hell are their cell phones?" Dap asked looking around the closet.

"Pops probably took the phones when he slumped them. I'm going back downstairs to find out what happened." Turning to leave the room, Dap grabbed my arm firmly snatching me back toward him.

"You slippin' nigga! We have to make this shit disappear and it must be done now! Do you think Uncle Spence will sacrifice his whip? It will be nothing to buy him a new one of his choice."

"Ay, Spence! Come here, Unc!" I yelled.

The sound of footsteps was heard thundering up the stairs and uncle Spence appeared in the doorway. "What's the matter, nephew?" he asked, peering around the room.

"I'm gon' need to use your car," Dap said without beating around the bush. "It's going to the chop shop afterwards so I'm prepared to buy whatever car you want in exchange."

"Dap, you don't have money like that to buy my dream car for me."

"Don't underestimate ya boy, Unc. I need you to go to Walmart and get two big tarps so we can move these bodies. Then leave the rest to us. Would you do that for me in less than thirty minutes? We've wasted enough time already and it's already damn near three o'clock in the morning."

"I'm on it," Spence said, turning to leave before he paused and faced us again. "Wes, go downstairs and listen to your wife. Your father is pretty upset, but just listen to him rant without saying anything out of the way to his anger. He is letting his feelings out on anybody that he can because he will be laying his wife to rest in a matter of days."

146

"I understand, and I'm going down now while you head to the store. I'm glad Pops was here to protect my wife."

"Protect your wife? Wes, them niggas was dead when we got here. Justice held this shit down herself. You got a soldier on your hands and baby girl ain't to be fucked with."

Spencer laughed and I didn't want to believe Justice handled the intruders on her own, but I'd seen her shoot a muthafucka and pull her strap without blinking. We made our way down the stairs and the conversation between Pops and my wife ceased immediately as Spence left the house. Taking a seat next to Justice, I took Faith from her arms. Inspecting my baby from head to toe, I made sure she didn't have a scratch on her.

As I glanced over at my wife, I noticed blood on the sleeve of her shirt. My heart started racing as I shifted Faith to my other arm.

"Baby, you're bleeding!" I exclaimed as I reached over to lift the hem of her shirt. "Are you alright?"

"I'm fine. I wanted to wait until you got here to take care of the situation before I went to the hospital. Pops examined the wound, cleaned it, and patched me up pretty good. The bullet went straight, through so it's not that bad."

"Tell me what happened, Jus," I said, caressing the bandage that covered her wound.

"About thirty minutes after you left, I was settling in bed with Faith when I heard the alarm chirp downstairs. I knew you weren't back that soon so while listening closely, I knew there was, in fact, somebody in the house. Grabbing Faith, I went straight to the safe room and strapped up," she said, sitting up on the sofa.

My father listened as she spoke, but kept his eyes on me. Justice cleared her throat before continuing her story. "I turned on the speaker to hear what they were talking about and I knew they were looking for me. I'm still trying to figure out why they were after me. I don't even know those guys. Baby, they were outside watching the house and saw when you left."

My father sat up and placed his elbows on his knees. "Why would anybody be watching your home, Wes? Other than Shanell, what else do you have going on? The guys I saw upstairs wouldn't have any affiliation with her at all. What have you done?"

"I ain't did shit! I don't know them muthafuckas! Pops, you're blaming me for this shit and it had nothing to do with me! What you gon' do is stop coming at me like I'm a muthafuckin' kid!"

"Hold up!" Dap interjected before things between my Pops and I got out of control. "This is about me. Justice was sought out to get at me. This has nothing to do with Wes or Shanell."

"That's not true, Dap." Justice reached for a phone on the table and handed it Dap after entering a code. "After I shot my way out of the safe room, I went through their pockets and found this," she said, handing the phone to Dap. "I have a feeling the female they're referring to is Shanell. There's nobody else who knows where Wes and I live."

Dap scrolled silently through the contents of the phone before saying anything. His brows furrowed and his top lip curled. "Lucci set this shit up and he has help. I don't know for a fact if it's Shanell, but like Justice said, nobody else knows where y'all lay ya head at night."

"Who the fuck is this Lucci person and why is he after you, son?" Pops cut in.

"Lucci is one of Rocco's sons. He feels Customs belongs to him because Rocco handed his jewelry business down to me and not them. Rocco was killed in his home back in Cali and Lucci and his brother did that shit. Now they are coming after me to get what they feel is rightfully theirs."

"Why am I just hearing about this? I should've known about it when you found out they were going to retaliate!"

"Pops, I had every intention of telling you about it, but Bria came home with Sage. With everything that took place afterwards, where was the time?" Dap asked. "I put my problems on the back burner to take care of my family, not to mention what happened to Tana."

"What happened to Tana? See, this shit has gotten out of hand and the two of you have been secretive about what the fucks been going on. I'm not about to be cleaning up y'all shit! There's no way

Justice should've been protecting herself against niggas that's gunnin' for y'all!"

"True enough, I played a part in what happened this morning, but what you're not going to do is imply that I put my family in harm's way. Fighting the battle with Shanell has been a task in itself and I'm out for blood with that. But I will take full responsibility with the shit that transpired with Lucci and his crew. My brother goes to war, I go to war."

Pops glared at me, but I put my hand up to stop whatever he planned to say. I had dealt with Shanell all wrong and gave her the opportunity to kill my mama. Mr. Nice Guy was gone. This shit had opened the door for me to avenge my mother's death at all cost.

"Listen to me. I have been trying to go about dealing with this situation the right way and it hasn't been working for me. That shit is dead. From this point on, I don't give a damn what happens, I'm putting an end to all this bullshit! We have all endured a tragic loss and it affected everyone in different ways. We will get through this together," I said while looking my father in his eyes.

"Losing ma hit you harder than the rest of us, Pops. That does not give you the right to scream at us for what's going on. Is it our fault? Absolutely. But we will get our lives back soon as we handle our business. I want to get through ma's homegoing first before we make any moves. What I'm gon' need you to do is sit back and let us deal with this."

"Wes, I'm not trying to chastise y'all, but I'm not sitting around twiddling my thumbs while all of this is going on. I've lost my wife, my daughter is in the hospital, and my grandson's been traumatized. Enough is enough! I'm in this fight with y'all. I have nothing to lose, both of you do."

"You have so much to live for, Dad," Justice said rising to her feet. "Don't ever think because Beverly is gone, there's nothing more to life. We all love you. Sit this one out. Be the best grandpa you can be while we take care of what's going on in the streets."

I cocked my head back and watched as Justice wrapped her arms around Pops' neck. I let her have her moment, but I caught on to the words she spoke. There was no way I'd let my wife cause havoc in the streets alongside me and my brother. She was a mother, and whatever she was doing back in the day, needed to stay where it was at.

"I appreciate you saying that, Justice, but I'm not sitting this one out. You aren't going to be in the mist of this shit either. Faith and Sage need you," Pops said, turning his attention back to me. "When we put my wife in that vault, we are going to tear this mutha-fucka up until all of your enemies are on the midnight train to hell."

The phone in Dap's hand started ringing and we all looked over at him. He shook his head no, and let it go into voicemail. It started ringing again and Dap hit the decline button to silence it.

"What you doing, bro? Answer that shit!" I yelled, startling Faith. Bouncing her on my knee, she settled down and nestled her head under my chin.

"If I would've answered, Lucci and the rest of his crew would be here in a blink of an eye. We don't need that shit right now. Spence needs to bring his ass on so we can dispose of these bodies."

Spence walked through the door struggling with one of the tarps. Dap pocketed the phone and rushed to help him get it up the stairs. "The other one is in the trunk of my car, go get it," Spence yelled over his shoulder.

Justice lifted Faith from my arms and headed for the stairs. I was assuming she was going to lay her in the nursery. Pops and I went out to the driveway and brought the second tarp inside. After locking the door, we moved up the stairs effortlessly to get the bodies wrapped up and out of my home.

It didn't take long for us to roll the bodies up and out of the house. What we did with them snake muthafuckas were irrelevant but they wouldn't be seen nor heard from again. When we got back to my home, the carpet was ripped up and the blood was cleaned off everything thoroughly.

Pops stayed at the house while Dap and I escorted Justice to the hospital. Sitting back as the doctor stitched her up, I went online to hit my realtor up so she could find a new crib for me and my family. Our home was not safe anymore and I was doing something to make sure mine was safe at all times.

Chapter 20

Bria

The day had arrived for us to lay my mother down to rest. I was released from the hospital the day before and I truly wasn't ready to say goodbye. My legs were still casted and I was in a wheelchair. The feeling of being incompetent was something I couldn't get with. Having my father taking care of me the way he did when I was younger was very weird. Sage was right beside him every step of the way.

Even though I did some dirty shit with Shanell and my brother and his wife suffered through her madness, Justice didn't stall to come help me get showered and dressed for my mother's service. Tana was there as well and they got my ass right in record time. As Justice styled my hair, I felt obligated to apologize to the both of them.

"Justice, thank you for coming over to help me. I know you want to beat my ass but I swear, I didn't know things would go the way they did with Shanell. I'm so sorry, and that is sincerely from the heart."

"Bria, today is not the day to address what Shanell has done. Apology accepted, but I want you know, that shit will not fly again. I want you to think before you act next time around. Nothing should ever come between you and family. Regardless of what happens, there is nothing and no one that should be able to lure you to the other side of the fence. Family is always first; no matter what."

Justice pointed the curling iron in her hand at my reflection in the mirror. "The most you can ever do is love the person from a distance, with a long stemmed spoon. But never turn your back on the ones that love you the most."

"I'm going to piggyback off what Justice said," Tana cut in. "Shanell is a grimy bitch who has done shit that she will never be able to come back from. Not only did she take Beverly from her family, she left a scar that may never heal. To be honest, I was ready to fuck you up myself but Justice beat me to the punch. Liking you is something I would have to work on.

"I'm willing to tolerate you because I love not only your brother, but this family as a whole. If I feel you're still in contact with Shanell, you will die right alongside of her. After this celebration, you have to explain everything to Sage. He didn't deserve to be lied to for the first five years of his life."

Tears rolled down my face and I was glad I opted not to wear makeup. It was the start of my waterfalls and it would be a long day of crying, but I would get it all out. Tana didn't say anything that wasn't truthful. She was correct about all she had said. Keeping the secret about Sage was the hardest thing I'd ever had to do in my life.

"That's fair. Shanell hasn't tried to contact me and vice versa. I honestly think Shanell believes I was killed the night she ran me over. As for Sage, Wes and I sat him down already and explained everything to him. It's not going to be easy for him to let go of the fact that I'm not his mother. We just have to take it day by day and see how it works out for him."

There was a knock on the door and Dap peeped his head inside. "Are y'all almost ready? The cars are here."

"Yeah, I have a few more curls and we will be right out," Justice said without stopping what she was doing.

"Hey, baby," my brother said, winking at Tana. "Come here so I can talk to you, beautiful."

"Nah, I'm not about to play with you, Donovan. Gon' head and get out of here." Tana laughed without moving.

"Aight, you gon' get caught up and I'm gon' catch yo' ass slipping. Remember that shit though." Closing the door with unnecessary force, Dap left the room.

"Bestie, he is going to tap that ass," Justice laughed. "Okay, Bria you're done. You ready roll up outta here?"

"No, I don't think I'll ever be ready for what I'm about to witness. There were supposed to be many more years to share between us. I regret holding the grudge for so long and now it's too late to even mend the bridge."

"Beverly forgives you, Bria. I'm sure she does. Let's get out of here before your daddy comes in to get us. All of that shit is squashed and we can work on getting to know one another," Justice said as she grabbed hold of the handles of my wheelchair.

Tana opened the door so she could wheel me out. My daddy, Wes, Dap, and Sage were sitting in the living room looking like quadruplets. My little baby had a deep frown on his face, but he kind of brightened up when we entered the room. Standing from his place on the sofa, he came over to me and hugged me tightly around the neck.

"I love you, Mommy. I'm ready to go see Grandma Bev," Sage said happily.

My dad told me he tried explaining death to Sage, but I'm seeing he still didn't really know what he was about to experience. All I could do was force a smile and place my dark glasses over my eyes. Justice joined Wes and Tana walked over to Dap, leaving me with my father as he pushed me out of the home I'd grown up in.

The ride to the church was quiet and seemed long. I was cool until the driver pulled into the parking lot. My breathing quickened; my heart started beating very fast. I couldn't catch my breath.

"Bria, here, drink this," Wes said, handing me a bottled water. "Breathe. You got this, sis."

After gulping down the water, I felt better, but when I glanced out of the window and laid eyes on the white hearse, reality really sat in. "I can't do this, y'all," I cried.

"Baby, you can and you will. If you don't do this, the regret you're already feeling is going to eat you up. This is the closure you need, Bria," my daddy said.

"We got you, sis. You will never be alone," Dap said, squeezing my hand as the back door opened.

There was a guy standing with my chair in front of his body. I didn't know who he was but the way he admired me, had my stomach feeling like a thousand butterflies were fluttering inside. His tattoos let me know he didn't work for the funeral home but it still left me wondering, who was he?

My brothers exited the vehicle first, followed by the women in their lives. Sage and my daddy got out, but he turned back and lifted me out of the car like I weighed nothing and then placed me in my chair. The unidentified guy pushed me toward the church and up the ramp. As I was rolled through the door and down the aisle, the open casket had me putting on the brake of my chair.

"Wait. Wait. Wait," I said with all eyes on me. The church was packed to capacity and there wasn't a dry eye in the building. "I can't do this!" I said a bit louder than before. The handsome guy that I was left with came around to face me and bent down until we were eye to eye.

"Bria, is it?" he asked, holding my hand as I shook my head up and down. "I'm Jamal, but everyone calls me Juice. I've been in your position and you need to confront this fear, ma. If you don't, it's gon' eat you up. I'm going to be here for you every step of the way. Dap put you in good hands and I got you."

"I can't—"

"There's nothing you can't do! Take that out of your vocabulary. I want you to cry, yell, whatever you need to do, get it out. Don't hold this hurt in, baby girl," Juice said, trying to comfort me.

Without much choice, I was pushed to the front of the church and my heart broke the closer I got to my mother. Trying my best to hold in my cries, I broke when I saw her lying motionless in her final bedding looking beautiful as ever. Sage was by my side and he was brave as he walked closer to the casket. Reaching his little hand inside, he pushed my mother's arm repeatedly.

"Grandma Bev, I'm back. Wake up! We can eat Coco Pebbles together." Sage looked around at all the people in the church before he turned back around to give one last attempt at trying to wake my mother. "Please wake up! Give me a hug, Grandma!" he wailed.

"She's not going to wake up, Sage!" I cried. At that moment, my family came to my aid and I lost it. "I'm so sorry, Mama! Please forgive me. I love you so much and I just want to hear you tell me you love me one more time!" Everything started moving rapidly around me before the room went black.

***

Unfortunately, I missed the rest of my mother's funeral because I blacked out. When I woke up, we were en route to my father's house. When we pulled up, there were so many cars lining both sides of the street and all I wanted to do was sleep. Both of my brothers carried me inside and placed me on the sofa in the living room. Pillows were placed under my legs to elevate them and I was comfortable.

"Bria, do you want something to eat?" Ms. Clara asked.

"No ma'am. I'm fine," I replied, turning my head to hide the tears that escaped my eyes.

"You have to eat something darling. I'll bring you a little bit so you can eat."

Ms. Clara walked away and I tuned everything out around me by closing my eyes and putting my arm over my face. I wanted all the people to leave so I could grieve in peace with the members of my family. Where were all of these folks when my mama was killed? Now everybody was so fuckin' concerned.

Sage was being introduced to members of the family that never knew he existed and he was glad to say he had a big family. I didn't want to be bothered, but I spoke whenever someone came over to tell me they were sorry for my loss. If I could get up on my own, walking out would've been the first move I made.

"Let me help you sit up so you can eat, ma."

Opening my eyes, I saw the handsome guy from earlier standing over me. "I'm not hungry, but thank you."

"I wasn't asking," he laughed. "You're going to eat. You don't need to be sick at a time like this."

"Why are you in such a need to come to my aid? I don't even know you."

"Look, my food is getting cold and these collard greens is looking too damn good for me to be playing around with you. A nigga hungry, ma."

"Well, eat. I'm not hungry and I won't eat until I'm ready."

Juice got the picture and pulled a chair up beside the sofa I was lying on and dug into his plate of food. The aroma filled my nostrils and my stomach growled lowly. Glancing at the plate he had set on the coffee table, I saw greens, mac and cheese, candied yams, ham, and dinner rolls calling my name.

"You ready to sit up?" Juice asked.

"I can probably eat a little bit."

"That's what I thought," he said, putting his plate down before helping me sit in an upright position. "How do that feel?"

"Fine. Now hand me the plate."

We ate in silence before he started a conversation and I felt comfortable enough to indulge him a little bit. I didn't know how much time had passed, but the last of the guests left out of the door and it was just the immediate family in the house. Sage came over and gave me a kiss on the cheek as he loosened his tie.

"Are you okay, Mommy?" he asked softly.

"Yes, baby, I'm alright. Sit down with me for a minute. There's something I want to talk to you about." Moving over a little bit, I patted the small space I created for him. Rubbing his back, I took a deep breath and smiled at him.

"I love you so much, Sage. You know that, right?"

"Yes, I know."

"Do you remember what we talked about the day you and grandpa came to the hospital?" Sage nodded his head yes and I continued speaking. "You have to practice calling me TeeTee Bria. I'm not your mommy, Sage. I was wrong for keeping the secret away from you and your daddy. I will forever be in your life, but I found your daddy for you. Isn't that what you wanted?"

Sage was quiet for a few seconds while Juice and I watched for his next move. He looked across the room at Wes and Faith and his head dropped. I waited until he was ready and didn't push him to talk.

"I'm glad Wes is my daddy, but if you can't be my mommy, who will be there to take your place? I don't want Auntie Nell to ever be my mommy."

156

Wes looked over at us and stood to his feet. "Sage, I know this is going to be hard for you to understand, son. Bria is your aunt and I'm your father."

"I know all of that, Uncle—I mean, Dad. Now that I know who you are, who's going to be my mama? At first, I didn't have a daddy. Now I don't have a mommy," Sage said with tears pooling in his tiny eyes.

"You will always have a mother. I may be Faith's mommy, but that's your little sister and I'm willing to be your mommy too," Justice said, sitting on the floor next to Sage.

Dap and Tana joined us followed by my dad and everyone was concentrating on Sage. The tears dropped rapidly from his eyes and he hurried to wipe them away. Justice gathered him in her arms and his little shoulders shook as he cried. Sage finally pulled back and sat back on the sofa.

"I've never had another mommy. I don't know what to do," Sage cried.

"Nephew, everything will be alright. Stop all that crying. Real men don't cry," Dap said from the loveseat.

"Does that mean you and my daddy aren't real men? Both of y'all was crying earlier today."

"That shit don't count, with ya educated ass. All I'm trying to tell you is everything is gon' be straight. Long as you have family, you have everything. It's not just you and Bria anymore. We got you, Sage. There's nothing for you to worry about."

"Okay. I need to take a nap. I'm going upstairs for a while." Sage gave hugs to everyone except Faith. He kissed her chubby cheek before making his exit.

"Bria, give him time. He'll come around. What are your plans? I want Sage here with me," Wes asked.

"I haven't thought about it, to be honest. I'll be here with Daddy until I heal, but I didn't have plans of taking Sage back to Michigan. He's your son, Wes, and you deserve to make a life with him."

"Sis, I think you should move back here. I will buy you a crib. I'll even make sure it's big enough for you to have enough room to run your business comfortably from home," Dap said.

"Dap, you're not in a position to buy me a house. I can't let you do that."

"I'm glad you don't know much about me, Bria. Ya bro is well off, and that means my family is too. We gon' look for you a crib and that's the end of it."

"Thank you, Dap. I was going to figure out how to move on my own, but I guess it's out of my hands now."

"So, it's settled then. We will all be together again."

"I guess so, Wes. I'm with Sage, I think I need a nap too. Today has taken a lot out of me. Can someone push my chair over, please?"

Handing Faith to Justice, Wes came over and picked me up in one swoop and headed to the guest bedroom down the hall. Laying me in the bed, he made sure I was comfortable and sat down beside me.

"Bria, we're going to be fine. When all of this bullshit is over, Dap and I will arrange to move all of your things back here."

"Mama looked beautiful today, Wes. I miss her so much."

"We all do, sis. Get some rest. I have some business to take care of and I'll be back to check on you. Thank you for being the best mother to Sage. You did a phenomenal job and whenever you decide to have kids of your own, you gon' nail that shit. You and Sage have a bond that can't be broken and I won't stand in the way of that, I promise."

"No thanks needed. I did what I thought was right at the time. I was wrong for not telling you, Wes. There's no way I'll ever be able to make up for the mistake I made. You missed out on so much of his life because of my choices."

"It's all good. I have a lifetime to go with Sage. This time, we can share memories together. How 'bout that?"

"Sounds like a plan. I love you, bro."

"I love you too, big head."

Wes kissed me on the forehead and left me staring at the ceiling. Thinking about my mama, I cried silently before drifting off to sleep.

Chapter 21

Shanell

I paced the floor of Lucci's hotel room. I had been there since meeting him. Not knowing where Dap lived, I gave him the next best thing, Wes' address. We came up with a plan of snatching Justice's ass up for ransom as the best solution. Wes would give anything to get that bitch back and it was perfect.

"Where the fuck is your people, Lucci? It's been days since they were sent to Wes' house and you haven't heard from them."

"Look, I know, bitch!"

"Bitch? You're the one that sent some weak ass Italians to do a job they couldn't handle. Lucci, you don't want to disrespect me because I'm not your average female. I would appreciate if you watched how the fuck you talked to me."

"Who the fuck you think you are? This is not the time for you to be running your dick suckers. I am in charge here! I will slap the hell out of you, Shan!"

Chuckling wildly, I looked Lucci up and down and then stopped laughing abruptly. "If you raise your hand to me, it will be the last time. I don't take threats lightly. Trust me, I will kill yo' ass in this muthafucka and leave you right here to bleed out."

"You're no match for me, Shan. Don't test me, bi—"

I was in his face faster than the speed of light with my box cutter up to his neck. "Go ahead and call me another bitch! Guttin' you like a fish would be easy," I gritted through my teeth. "I've killed so many people it's a job now. Don't fuck with me, *bitch*!"

As I dug the tip of the blade in Lucci's neck, his phone chimed. Stepping back so he could tend to his business, I kept the blade in my hand in case he wanted to retaliate. Lucci backed up and all I saw was his dick swinging in his pajama pants. The mind-blowing sex came to mind and my kitty started purring. I wanted him badly, but after damn near ending his life, I didn't think he would feed me what I needed at the moment.

"It's Franco. He said they missed the target."

"What, it took days for them to say they missed? Something isn't right with that," I said, sitting on the bed. "Why would they wait so long to tell you?"

"Both of them know I don't tolerate botched jobs. Waiting just cost them their lives and they know this. They would rather run than face me."

"That's bullshit, Lucci! Text something back that only he would know. I have a feeling it's not Franco, or whatever his name is, that's responding."

"I will do one better. I'll call."

Lucci called Franco's phone and waited to see if he would answer. He put it on speaker and we both listened until the call finally connected. The sound of someone breathing could be heard, but no words were spoken.

"Franco, what the hell happened? How did you fuck up a simple job?"

"You sent the wrong muthafuckas; that's how!" Dap's voice roared through the speaker. "When you come for the Kings, you have to think twice about the Queens, Lucci." Dap laughed. "What's your next move, sucka? By the way, tell Shanell I said hello. Don't trust that bitch, Lucci. She's a wolf in sheep's clothing. Shanell will turn on you quick as fuck."

Lucci glanced up before responding. "Who the fuck is Shanell? I sent Franco and Piero to take care of the bitch."

"And she was underestimated. You can't send a boy to do a man's job. Shid, you niggas gon' fail every time y'all come for one of mine. Far as Shanell goes, if you fucked her, she's about to be on yo' ass like a leech on skin. Now that's the bitch you need to watch your back for. Don't trust her. She's crazier than a bitsy bug."

"I'm not crazy, Dap!" I fucked around and revealed myself and I regretted it the minute the words left my mouth.

"Shanell, Shanell, Shanell! I knew I'd be able to get you to show your face. You know you fucked up, right? Killin' Beverly was the wrong thing for you to do. Suck in all the air you can because these are your last days, bitch. You took something away from this family that we can't get back. You gon' pay for that shit."

160

"Your whole family paying for it, pussy! I will forever be in y'all thoughts," I laughed.

"Laugh now, cry later. You two muthafuckas teamed up at the right time. Checkmate! See you muthafuckas soon."

"Fuck! How the hell did he know you were working with me?" Lucci screamed.

"They are slow, not stupid. You don't know shit about Chicago. You had to have help. I'm the only other person that has beef with them niggas. It wasn't hard for them to put two and two together. Let me find out you scared."

"I'm not scared of anybody! Don't fuckin' try to antagonize me!"

"Calm yo' ass down and come put that dick down my throat. We have to fuck this anger out because we have to think about our next move. I can't think on an empty pussy," I said, dropping to my knees.

***

There was a knock on the door and I rolled over to an empty bed. The sun was going down as I looked out the window, admiring the beautiful scene. Lucci walked in pushing a cart and I sat up in the bed, letting the cover fall, exposing my breasts.

"Get up and put on some clothes. Fuckin' is the last thing I want to do right now. My dick is sore. We need to figure out how we're going to get at Dap before he comes for us," he said, bringing a plate that consisted of steak, a loaded potato, and broccoli with cheese sauce. Taking a huge spoonful of the potato, I chewed with my eyes closed.

"You're too late for that. You were on that call for about four minutes and I will bet the little bit of money I have in my account the call was traced."

"Dap is not that smart. He doesn't have the power to trace shit! He wouldn't have half of what he got if it wasn't for my father! He's a dumbass that relies on others to help him succeed."

"There you go underestimating a black man. I give credit where it is due and Donovan King is far from dumb. He is street smart, Lucci. That's more powerful than anything he has done business wise. I know the man behind the business," I said, savoring the taste of the steak. "Your father didn't teach him that shit. The streets of Chicago were the leader in that department."

"Whatever! He owes me and I'm going to get what's mine."

"I hear you, but he is three steps ahead of you. We have to get out of this hotel and into another because he already knows where we are. Leaving won't guarantee we'll be safe, but we would have a fair chance of surviving another day."

"Do you know how to shoot?" Lucci asked out of the blue.

"I do, but my specialty is stabbing a muthafucka. Why do you ask?"

Lucci reached in the top drawer and held out a .22 caliber. I laughed, licking my fingers and moving the tray to the side. I walked over to my purse and removed a nine-millimeter.

"I can't do anything with that lil shit. I'll be cool with my bitch."

"Okay, you burned down Customs, so where is another place we can find Dap?" Lucci asked.

"Wes probably has the family heavily guarded. It's going to be pretty hard to touch them now. The only thing we can do is sit back and wait for them to come for us. Otherwise, we will be dead before we can blink good if we try to run into another one of their houses."

"Waiting is something I refuse to do. I know for a fact Franco and Piero are dead. That leaves me with only six on my team, including you and myself. I'm no longer hungry," he said, rising from the foot of the bed. "I'm going to talk to my brother and the rest of the team. I'll be back later."

Watching Lucci leave the room, I finished my food and his too. I was hungry as hell. After placing the dishes on the cart, I pushed it outside the door and went searching through Lucci's shit. His ass had a shitload of money that I took the liberty of helping myself to. It was payback for all I was sacrificing to help him.

I went into the bathroom and took a long hot shower, and then put on a green Nike jogging suit with a pair of green and white sneakers. I pulled my hair into a ponytail and grabbed the extra room key and my purse before walking to the door. I shot Lucci a text and told him to be ready to vacate the hotel in an hour. There was no way I was about to wait on him to decide when we would move around.

Meesha

Chapter 22

Dap

Two days after answering the phone call Lucci placed to Franco's phone, I had Christian track that muthafucka's line and had a hit before I hung up. Shanell was in cahoots with Lucci and I was excited because I would be able to hit Lucci, his team, and her ass at the same damn time. Setting everything up, I was already sitting outside when Shanell made her exit from the hotel. Following her was easy because the bitch forgot about the golden rule of paying attention to her surroundings.

I waited as she got out of her car and entered the Radisson Blu Aqua hotel. It wasn't too far from the hotel they were staying in before, but it was good for me because they were closer to the lake. That was where some of them were going to end up fuckin' with me. Shanell emerged from the hotel and I followed her around while she blew money like she had it like that. Letting her live her best life, I branched off as she entered the Coach store.

Hitting Christian's name in my phone, I got on the expressway and hit the gas as I waited for the call to connect. "What's up, Dap?"

"Yeah, Shanell's ass just checked into the Radisson. I got Tools and Kato keeping watch at Whitehall. We are going to make our move soon. They know to scoop whichever one of them niggas emerge first. I'm on my way to check out the spot my pops got right now. I'll make sure everything is ready because Lucci and Arturro is gon' pay for the shit they did to Rocco."

"All you got to do is hit my line. I'll be ready for whatever."

"Bet."

Ending the call, I cruised southbound on the Dan Ryan passing 35th Street. "Damn" by YoungBloodz boomed through the speakers of my ride and it fit right with my mood.

If you don't give a damn, we don't give a fuck
If you don't give a damn, we don't give a fuck
If you don't give a damn, we don't give a fuck
Don't start no shit, it won't be no shit

Don't start no shit, it won't be no shit
Don't start no shit, it won't be no shit
Don't start no shit, it won't be no shit

I pulled in front of the warehouse that my father had given me the keys to and cut off the engine. It was a spot he owned, but never did anything with. I wanted to see what I was working with because a torture chamber was what I had in mind. Approaching the metal door as I pulled the key from my pocket, the sound of a car's engine had me automatically reaching for my tool. I turned toward the sound and my pops was pulling alongside of my ride.

"Yo' ass was slow as fuck," Pops said, getting out of his car. "You were a goner, son, if it was someone out to hurt you."

"What you doing here, old man?"

"I was trying to get here before you to see what the conditions of this place were like. It's been awhile since I've stepped foot in this bad boy," Pops said, walking around me inserting a key into the lock. "You didn't think I gave you the only key, did you?" He smirked, pushing the metal door open.

We walked in and I was in awe because everything I envisioned was right before my eyes. There were chains already mounted in the ceilings, a chair was sitting in the middle of the floor with chains and cuffs already attached, there were chainsaws and knives, there was a coffin like box with nails on the inside, and so much more. To my left there was a hole in the floor with what looked like swamp water in it. The wheel that was mounted to the wall had metal clamps connected to it to bind someone's wrists and ankles together. A nigga was like a kid in the candy store with all this shit.

"Pop, what the hell you doing with a place like this?" I asked, walking further into the warehouse.

"It's a little something I kept in tiptop shape from when I was deep in these streets."

"Deep in the streets? This shit looks like it's been used every day. None of the equipment is even rusty."

"When Beverly was murdered, I needed something to get my mind off what I lost. Plus, I knew you would need somewhere to handle the business without bringing any attention to yourself. So I came and fixed shit up, just in case. Go take a look at what I bought in the very last room on the right."

As I made my way to the room Pops spoke of, loud growls could be heard coming from the other side of the door. I won't lie; my ass was scared to open that muthafucka. The sound of Pops laughing made me turn to face him to see what the hell was so funny.

"Just open the door with your chickenshit ass."

"Man, it sounds like a zoo behind this door. You open it then," I said, stepping to the side so he could do the honors.

"Move your punk ass out the way." Pops elbowed me further away from the door and turned the knob and pushed the door open. "There you go with yo' scary ass. Meet your new friends."

Peeking inside the room, I saw four white Siberian tigers in big-ass cages. They were kind of small in weight, but that didn't take from how big they were. Pops stepped in the room and the tigers stood on all four legs, ready to attack.

"Why the hell do you have these anorexic ass tigers, Pops?"

"They are just what we need to get rid of any evidence in the crimes we are about to commit. These tigers haven't been fed in months and they hungry as fuck. Wild animals are their food of choice, but I bet they won't turn down human flesh if given to them."

"Damn, big homie. I don't know what you were into back in the day, but remind me not to get on your bad side." I laughed, backing out of the room.

"You're safe, son," he laughed. "All I got to do is knock you on your ass a little bit and you'll be back in line in no time."

"I keep trying to tell you, I'm not the same lil kid you used to whoop. I can keep up with you now, Pops."

"Get yo' ass shot if you want to. Let's get out of here," he said, walking back to the front of the warehouse. "Don't forget to call me soon as you have action. I can't wait to feed those tigers. I don't care what else y'all do. I have to feed the cats."

"It's all yours, man. I'm not about to be fileting no damn humans. You can have all that shit," I laughed as he locked up. Walking to my ride, my phone started ringing and I hurried to get it out of my pocket. "What up, Kato?"

"Ay, we got Arturro in the trunk, where you want him?"

"Bring his ass to the address I'm about to send you. I'll be waiting."

"Say no more. I'm on the way."

Ending the call, I turned to my Pops before he could get inside his ride. "Today must be your lucky day, old man. We got our first round of bait. You ready for this shit?"

"Hell yeah! Let me get suited up. I know you gon' want to interrogate the muthafucka first." He laughed, slamming the door and walking back to the warehouse.

I'd waited my whole life for this shit. Arturro was about to wish his father was still breathing and he had stayed in a child's place.

***

It took Kato and Tool about forty minutes to arrive at the warehouse. They didn't know shit about Chicago and the GPS was taking them around the world. Kato called me and I had to guide them to the warehouse, turn by turn. When he told me they were pulling up, I walked outside dressed in a plastic suit.

"What the fuck you got going on?" Tool asked, getting out of the whip.

"You'll see once y'all get inside. Bring his ass in."

Kato and Tool stood at the trunk of the ride with guns drawn. I could hear Arturro kicking the inside of the trunk, trying to scream out, but his cries were muffled. Tool punched his ass so hard when the trunk was opened, I heard it from the doorway.

"Shut the fuck up, bitch!" he snapped, snatching Arturro's legs outward.

Kato grabbed his upper body and brought him out of the car. Arturro was jerking his body wildly but it didn't stop my niggas from getting him inside without incident.

"Put his ass in that chair and strap him in that muthafucka tightly. He's about to learn today."

Arturro was trying to scream his ass off as he was placed in the chair that was bolted to the floor. I stalked over to him and snatched the tape from his mouth, ripping his mustache off along with it.

"Arrrrghhh!" He bucked, trying to free himself from the restraints. "Dap, why are you doing this shit, mane?"

"Why am I doing this? Nigga, you muthafuckas crossed a line that y'all can't come back from! I have a question for you, and you got one chance to answer it truthfully," I said, standing in front of him. "Why did y'all have to kill Rocco?"

Arturro's eyes expanded out of the sockets and he glanced erratically around the open space. I knew off top he was trying to figure out how to answer the question, but I was a patient nigga. The lie was coming and I was ready for it.

"We had nothing to do with that, I swear to God."

I punched his ass in the jaw. His head swiveled to the side and blood spurted from his mouth. "You a muthafuckin' lie! It was money! I was told early on that money was the root of all evil and you and Lucci proved that shit! Rocco left you muthafuckas money in his will, but because you didn't get the bulk of it, y'all killed him! Guess what though? Neither one of you bitches will see a dime of it!"

I stared down at Arturro, and his face swelled before my eyes. He puckered his lips to spit and I hit his ass again, punching him until my knuckles ached. One of his front teeth connected with my fist and the pain shot up my arm, causing me to end the attack.

"You got it all wrong," he struggled to say through bruised lips. "I know all about my father leaving me and Lucci money. The amount was sufficient for me. My brother wasn't satisfied with our father giving us pennies when we asked, so he came up with the plan to get rid of him and collect the insurance money. I wanted no parts of it."

Arturro was lying through the teeth he had left. If he had nothing to do with the plan at all, why was he in Chicago on bullshit with the muthafucka? I wanted to hear his side of the story because

I wanted to see how much he was going to put on Lucci. Arturro would've gotten a little more respect from me if he would've just told the truth, but he decided to lie and it only made it that much worse for him.

"Lucci contacted the lawyer and found out we were only getting a hundred grand apiece. We didn't understand how Father was a billionaire, but the two of us were receiving so little."

"You muthafuckas are lucky to get that much! The love your father had for y'all went unnoticed because all y'all saw was dollar signs. I was more of a son to Rocco than his own kids! I'll tell you why only two hundred thousand total was given to his living sons. It's because he had more faith in a nigga that didn't have the same blood running through his veins than his own offspring's.

I'm the billionaire, muthafucka! I will be the one carrying on his legacy because you two pussies weren't built to do the job! It's not that he didn't try to mold y'all to take over. Neither one of you would sit down long enough to learn what he was trying to teach. And that's one of the reasons you're about to die today."

Walking across the room to the tools hanging on the wall, I removed a sledgehammer from the hook and gripped it tightly in both of my hands. Silently apologizing to Rocco, I approached Arturro and swung with all my might, shattering his left kneecap.

"Arrrrghhhh! Oh my God! I'll tell you where Lucci is, just spare my life!" he screamed out.

"Spare your life? Nigga, you were dead the moment I received the call that you had been dumped in the trunk. Did you give Rocco the opportunity to add more zeros to the amount you would receive in his will? Hell nawl, you didn't. I don't know the meaning of mercy and I'm not going to practice on yo' ass tonight. Fuck you!"

Swinging the sledgehammer again, I connected with Arturo's head. His brain matter came out of his ear and leaked out of the hole that I created in the top of his head. Arturo's body slumped to the side and I knew he was dead from the fatal blow. Bad as I wanted him to suffer, I couldn't tolerate all the begging and pleading he had started to do.

Pops emerged from the back of the warehouse with an electrical saw in his hand. Kato and Tools removed the cuffs from around Arturo's arms and legs. His body fell forward and hit the concrete floor with a thud. Pops started cutting his limbs off one by one and I had to turn my back because I wasn't into that bullshit at all. When the saw stopped, I waited a full fifteen minutes before I turned back around.

The clothing that Arturro was wearing sat on top of a blood puddle. I walked to the sink and turned on the hose. Spraying the blood toward the drainage hole, I watched it disappear very quickly. Adding a bit of bleach and ammonia to the surface, I washed away all signs of anything ever happening in the space. Pulling on a pair of gloves, I gathered all the pieces of clothing and took them to the furnace room, where Pops had already started it up. I threw everything inside and waited for Pops to come back from the back.

"That shit was wild! Those big muthafuckas still hungry. I've never seen nothing like that in my life. This just made a believer out of me with that *Tiger King* shit. That bitch fed her husband to that to that damn cat. Ain't no way I'm going to say it's impossible because I witnessed it with my own eyes!"

Kato was excited as hell as he walked towards me. "D, you missed that shit, man!" he said, clapping his hands.

"Let's go. I don't want to hear shit about it. There's other shit to be done, but it won't happen today. Yo' ass done had enough excitement for one day. I'm going home to my woman to clear my head. Thanks for helping end one muthafucka's life."

"You alright, son?"

"Yeah, I'm good, Pops. I just need to get out of here," I said, walking out of the warehouse.

Opening the door to my ride, I got in and cranked up the engine. The phone connected to the Bluetooth immediately and I scrolled through my call log. I hit Christian's name, and the phone rang as I backed out onto the street.

"Dap, how's things going? I haven't been able to track Lucci's phone, and—"

171

"That's not what I'm calling about, Unc." I cut him off before he could get started. "I wanted to inform you that I caught up with Arturro. Things didn't go well for him and I wanted to apologize for what I had to do."

"My nephews brought this shit on themselves. Arturro deserved what he got and I don't feel sorry for him. Lucci is next because my brother didn't deserve what happened to him. Dap, don't ever apologize to me or the next man for handling what needed to be handled. I have nothing but respect for you. We will forever be family."

"I wanted you to hear it from me. Thanks for standing by me. We will have to get together soon before you take off for the west coast."

"I'm all for it. I'm enjoying this city you live in, Dap. The food is good and the pussy is even better. Leaving isn't on my to-do list until one of us finds Lucci. I know he is still roaming around and he's going to pop up eventually. Just keep your eyes open."

"Will do. I'll get at you soon. But hit my line the minute you get movement on Lucci's ass."

Christian agreed to contact me and my mind was on getting home to love on my woman. I hit the gas and sped toward my house to get the best stress reliever on the market, and her name was Tana.

Chapter 23

Wes

"Baby, Stewart is on the phone!" Justice yelled from the top of the basement stairs.

For the past three weeks, I'd been in my mancave if I wasn't out in the street searching high and low for Shanell and Lucci. After Dap killed Arturro, we were able to catch three of his henchmen living it up at the strip club. Eliminating them left the two of them on the loose. Christian could no long track their phones because obviously they had disposed of them. But they could only hide for so long. Their time would come eventually.

"Come on down, babe." Justice handed my phone to me and turned to walk away. I pulled her into my lap and kissed the back of her neck. "I love you," I whispered in her ear.

"I love you too," she responded as she turned her head and kissed me tenderly on the lips. "I'll be back." As I watched my wife climb the stairs, I finally addressed Stewart on the phone.

"What's good, Stew?"

"Wes, my man! How's everything going?"

"Everything is everything, man. So much has gone on that I don't know which way I'm going, to be honest."

"The boss asked me to call to see when you would be back in the office. He feels you've been gone long enough and he needs you back to work."

"Check this out, Stew. Before everything happened with my family, I had over three hundred paid time off hours and over ninety days of vacation days. I haven't put a dent in either one. Laying my mother to rest was the hardest task I've ever had to do in my life. If Williamson has a problem with me being out of the office, tell his ass to hit me up personally because I'm not coming back anytime soon."

"King, I don't want you to lose your job over this. Come in and talk with Williamson and straighten this shit out."

"I've been talking to him and Human Resources via e-mail and submitted everything needed for my time off. If Williamson wants to let me go, I'll be good until I find another place of employment. What I won't do is bow down because he wants me to grieve on his time. That's not the way it works with me. One thing for sure, he will be paying me for every hour and day for PTO and vacation days."

"I'm sorry about your mom, King. I'll keep in touch and you should hear from Williamson soon. To be honest, things haven't been right around here since you've been out. I believe that's why he's trying to pressure you to come back sooner than later."

"Stew, that's on him. Citywide is his company and he should be able to keep it afloat on his own. Tell his ass to call me because I won't be calling him. I'll talk to you soon."

I'd spent almost five years working for Citywide and the inconsideration of Williamson just blew the fuck out of me. I'd rather bust my ass on my own before I allow anyone to force me to make a choice between my family and a job. My phone lit up and I had an e-mail notification from the realtor I had hired to find Justice a new home.

As I read the message, I smiled because she had found two houses and wanted me to view them both. I sent a quick reply and agreed to meet her at the first location within the hour. Since she found properties not too far away from where we currently resided, that was a major plus for me. Dap was still in the area and I wanted to be close to him since he chose his own home to be closer to me. As I climbed the steps to the main floor of my home, I placed a call to Dap.

"What's up, brah?"

"You at the crib?" I asked.

"Yeah. You need me?"

"Sure do. I want to go check out these houses for my baby. You rollin'?"

"How many do you have on the list?"

"Two, and they aren't too far away."

"Bet, I'll be ready when you pull up. Or do you want me to meet you?"

"Nah, I'll be through in a minute."

"Aight, one."

Faith's laughter filled my ears as I rounded the corner. She was getting so big and looked more like Justice every day. As soon as Faith saw me, her arms went straight up in the air and she started crawling up Justice's back to get to me.

"Hey, Daddy's baby," I said, swooping her up. I played with Faith for about ten minutes, but I knew I had to get out and meet the realtor. "Babe, I'm about to go take care of some business. You need anything?"

"No, I'm about to get started on dinner. Dad is coming over with Bria and Sage."

"Oh, okay. I'll be back before then but make sure it's enough food for Dap and Tana because once he finds out everyone will be here, his ass will be coming through too."

"Tana already knows," Justice laughed. "She'll be over any minute to help."

I took the phone from my pocket to call my brother, but the doorbell chimed before I could press the button. When I snatched the door open, Tana was standing on the porch looking like she had swallowed a baby watermelon and Dap was walking up the driveway. His ass was going to get cussed out if he would've stayed at the house waiting for me to pick his ass up.

"Heyyyyy, Faye Faye," Tana sang, reaching for Faith.

"Damn, hello, Tana."

"Boy, shut up. My baby gets all the love from me. But how you doing?"

"Nah, your moment has passed, move along," I said, stepping aside to let her into the house. "Baby, I'm about to roll out. I won't be gone too long."

"Weston King, I wish you would leave without giving me some suga." Justice pouted, standing with her hands on her hips.

"Come here, Shawty." She ran to me and jumped into my arms, covering my face with wet, sloppy kisses. When she finally kissed my lips, our tongues danced and my pipe swelled instantly.

"Man, take that shit upstairs! Don't nobody want to witness all that," Dap's hating ass snarled.

"I love you, baby. Hurry back," Justice said, walking away with an extra swing in her hips. Stopping mid step, she turned back around and smirked at Dap. "Don't be jealous because we got that love thing going on, bro. I'll talk to Tana and tell her to step her game up." Laughing at the expression on my brother's face, I closed and locked the door before I walked to my ride.

"Wes, something is wrong with Justice. You better get her checked to make sure she's not crazy like Shanell's ass," Dap said, opening the passenger door.

"She's just fuckin' with you, bro. Get your panties out ya ass. The only way her teasing hit a nerve is if you and Tana is having problems."

"To be honest, Tana hasn't wanted me to really touch her since she came home from the hospital. I believe that nigga Tyson raping her kind of fucked her up. I've been living with blue balls for over a month."

"Damn, I don't think Justice knows about that. If she did, she would've never spoke on it. Give Tana time. I'm sure she will come around," I said, starting the car.

"Enough about that. We have to find Shanell and Lucci. They've been moving freely and probably with no care in the world. I've actually been thinking that they're plotting something big. Fife and Juice have been watching the hotel and there hasn't been any movement in weeks. Shanell's car hasn't moved out of the hotel parking lot so I believe they have gotten away again."

Thinking about what Dap said, I picked up the phone and called the Radisson hotel. There was one way to find out if Shanell was still staying there with Lucci. Waiting for someone to answer the phone, I backed out of my driveway and headed for the first house. The realtor had texted both addresses to my phone briefly after we agreed to meet up.

"Thank you for calling Radisson Hotel, this is Julie speaking, how may I help you?"

"Hi Julie, this is Albert Jones. I'm trying to reach my sister, Shanell Jones. I dropped her off there and she said she would be staying at the hotel until her home was ready. It's been hard contacting her on her cell phone, so would you be a doll and go to her room for a wellness check?"

"I'm sorry to hear that, Mr. Jones. What room is your sister in?" Julie asked.

"She never told me her room number." The sound of Julie tapping away on the keyboard could be heard.

"Mr. Jones, unfortunately Shanell Jones checked out of the hotel a few weeks ago actually. If you're not able to contact her, in my opinion, you should contact law enforcement if you think she's in danger."

"No, no that won't be necessary. Maybe her house was ready sooner than expected. I know where she may be. Thank you so much for checking. Enjoy the rest of your day."

"No problem." I glanced over at Dap and he shook his head.

"I talked to Christian earlier and he hasn't had any luck tracking Lucci either. Both of them definitely dumped their phones. As of now, we gon' have to play this shit by ear. If my gut feeling is right, Shanell and Lucci are going to come to us. We just have to be ready. I'm going to move my crew out here to my crib. I'll have them posted up in the front and back of your crib, and one of them in the crib with Pops, Bria, and Sage."

"That sounds like a plan, but what about yo' shit?"

"Shanell don't know shit about me other than the location of Customs."

"How are the renovations coming along?"

"They're going great, actually. Everything will be complete in a few months. Hell, after the insurance claim, I got back more than what I put into the building when I bought it the first time around. You already know I'm going all out this time. Plus, the two stores that were destroyed in the fire collected their money and bounced. Customs is about to be big as fuck."

"That's good, bro. I knew you were going to come back strong. Nothing is going to stop you from getting where you are destined to be. I'm proud of you. We've been through so much in the past few months and you still coming up on top," I said pulling into the driveway of a big-ass brick house.

"Damn, bro. This house is huge!"

"Man, tell me about it. I hope it's as good on the inside. Let's check it out."

We got out and walked up the stairs. Dap reached out to ring the doorbell but it was snatched open by a sexy woman that looked like a Nubian Queen. Baby girl was dressed from head to toe in African garments and she wore that shit well. If I wasn't married, I'd definitely hit that.

"Mr. King?" Her voice was sultry and the way she said "King" sounded like a lullaby.

"Yes," both me and Dap replied in unison.

"Nice to meet you both," she smiled. "I'm Blessing Knox and this house is a beauty."

"Yes, you are," Dap said with his eyes roaming over her body. "You are a blessing and beautiful, Queen."

I elbowed his ass in the ribs because even though Tana wasn't giving up the pussy, he still had a pregnant woman at home.

Miss Knox stepped to the side and allowed us to enter. The first thing that captured my attention was the huge bay windows when we stepped into the first room off the entryway.

"There are five bedrooms, three baths, a finished basement, and a laundry room. This is what they would call a sitting room, but there's actually a living room further into the home. They're both about the same size, so you have a choice of what you would like to do with it."

Blessing guided us to the kitchen and there were stainless steel appliances, marble tabletops, and a walk-in pantry. My mother would've loved to get down in there. I shook the thought of my mother from my head so I wouldn't get emotional. I liked what I saw so far with the house.

"How many bedrooms are on this level?" I asked.

"Two. The other three are upstairs. I'll wait down here while you guys look around."

I went straight for the basement to see how my mancave looked. As I descended the stairs, I saw that the room was much bigger than the one at our current home and I was ready to make it my own. That space alone had me sold on the crib. Dap went upstairs and he would tell me what that shit was like, but I was putting a down payment on it today.

Blessing was standing by the island when I entered the dining area and I nodded my head. "I want it."

"Are you sure, Mr. King? You haven't been upstairs or outside yet."

"Trust me, I want this house."

Dap came downstairs with a smile on his face. "Brah, this house is the shit. Sexy Blessing, we will take it! There's a balcony in the master bedroom and the view into the backyard is amazing. Did you see the big-ass pool in the back?" This nigga was more excited than I was and he wasn't the one that would be living there.

"I've already came to that conclusion." I laughed. "I still want to see the other crib though," I said, turning to Blessing. "How many bedrooms does the other house have?"

"That house is smaller and it has three bedrooms. I just added it to the list just in case this one was too big for your liking."

"Bria. We can check it out to see if it would be good for her," Dap said, reaching inside his coat pocket. "Let's get this paperwork going so I can get back to yo' crib to eat."

Blessing walked to the end of the island and opened a manila folder. "Your down payment will be four thousand—"

"How much is the sale price on this house?" Dap asked.

"It's going for three hundred seventy-five thousand. The nineteen-thousand-dollar deposit will make the payments lower each month."

"I'm going to put down twenty thousand instead," I replied, taking the blank check from my pocket.

"Nah, brah. I got this." Dap started scribbling in his checkbook and then ripped it out, handing it to Blessing. Her eyes got big as saucers before she looked up at him. "I know you work on commission and I don't want you to wait to receive it."

"What the hell did you do? That check better be for twenty thousand dollars," I snapped.

"Nah, you don't need to be worried about making payments every month. This is my gift to you. Just take it, brah."

"We'll talk about this later, but I'm not going to allow you to buy me a home without me putting any money into it," I said, letting him know his idea wasn't sitting well with me. "Thank you, Blessing. I love the house."

"You're more than welcome, Mr. King. I'll have the paperwork drawn up for you in a few days. Once that's completed, you and your family can start the big moving process." Blessing, gathered her things and followed us to the door. "You guys can trail me to the next property. It's not too far away."

Without responding, Dap and I headed to my whip and waited until Blessing was settled in her car. "Damn, she's fine as fuck. Tana has to slob on my shit before I end up buying a house just because," Dap said, licking his lips while staring at Blessing.

Chapter 24

Tana

"Girl, your man is probably mad at me." Justice laughed, entering the kitchen.

"Why, what happened?"

"Wes and I were tonguing each other down and he told us to take that shit somewhere else. I responded saying I would tell you to step your game up. If looks could kill, I'd still be lying on the floor."

I paused for a second and felt bad because I had been neglecting Dap in the sexual department. It had nothing to do with him, but everything to do with what Tyson had done to me. I prayed every day that I would be able to overcome the situation, but I didn't see it happening anytime soon. The entire encounter scarred me and hopefully it wouldn't be for life.

"What's the matter, Tana?" Justice asked, walking over to where I was sitting at the table.

"Dap probably thought I mentioned we haven't been intimate," I stated sadly. "It's been so hard for me to accept him sexually since the incident with Tyson. Justice, I feel so dirty at times."

"Damn, Tana. Why didn't you tell me? Tyson is a piece of shit and I can't wait for his ass to come up missing. I'm sorry he violated you the way he did, but Dap loves you. I won't stand here and tell you to bust it open for him because it's not that easy. You will come around in your own time and hopefully Dap understands what you're going through. Talk it out with him. That would be better than avoiding the situation."

"I'm afraid if I don't start pleasing him, he's going to go out and get it elsewhere." A lonely tear escaped my eye and I tried to wipe it away before Justice noticed. Unfortunately, I wasn't quick enough.

"Aht, aht! Don't think that way. I see how Dap looks at you and stepping out is the last thing on his mind. If anything, he is trying to find the people responsible for what happened here and trying to get

Customs back up and running. Stop all the negative thinking and concentrate on staying healthy for the baby and getting back to yourself."

"I hear you. I'm ready to get this meal on the table. What are we cooking?" I asked, changing the subject.

"I figured I'd keep things simple. A pot of spaghetti, fried chicken, and corn muffins. By the time Wes gets back, everything should be ready. I'm not trying to be in this kitchen for too many hours."

Justice and I moved around the kitchen getting everything on the stove. About an hour later, the doorbell rang and I wiped my hands on a dish towel and went to answer the door. Looking out the front window, I spotted my father-in-law's car and Justice snatched the door open.

"Heyyyyy, Justice!" Sage shrieked as he ran full speed ahead with his arms outstretched.

"Hello, big boy! How ya been?" I stepped aside to allow Wes Sr., Bria and Juice inside.

"Boy, let her go so we can get some love too," Wes Sr. said as he leaned in for a hug. "Where's your big head husband? Hey, Tana," he said, giving her a hug after releasing Justice.

"He and Dap went out to conduct some type of business. Hey, Bria and Juice."

Bria was walking with a cane since the doctor had taken the casts off her legs. The rehabilitation looked as if it was really progressing her walking abilities and that was a good thing. Juice had been by her side since the day of Beverly's funeral and I think he had fallen for Bria, but I wasn't sure.

"It smells good in here," Bria said, easing past Sage, who had yet to let go of Justice's waist. Juice nodded his head and gave me a quick side hug and followed Bria into the living room. Justice looked down at Sage and shook her head.

"Okay, Sage. Let me go so I can close the door."

"I'll do it for you!" he said excitedly as he turned to do just that. "Where's Faith?"

On cue, Faith started fussing from the playpen Justice had placed her in while she was doing the cooking. Sage ran across the room to tend to her like the little protector he was. When he ran past Bria, who was sitting on the couch, I knew he was about to get fussed at.

"Sage, what have I told you about running?"

"Ewww, Justice, she stinks," Sage said, approaching the play-pen.

"Go upstairs and get a diaper and the wipes. And Sage…walk," Justice called out to him as she made her way across the room. I sat next to Wes Sr. on the couch.

"You alright, Tana?" he asked softly.

"Yeah, I am fine. Just a little tired from slaving in the kitchen with Justice."

"Girl, stop lying. You sat most of the time and I'm not even mad at you. I know what it feels like to be pregnant, so I let you be great."

"Whatever! Give me my Faye Faye so I can see what's taking this boy so long to get two items."

Climbing the stairs, I got to the top of the stairs and Sage still hadn't come out of the nursery. Entering the room, I started laughing because Sage was struggling to hold an armful of diapers and the wipes. The diapers kept falling to the floor and he groaned, stomping his feet. Everything fell out of his arm and he was big mad.

"Dammit!"

"Now watch your mouth and pick everything up. You were asked to come up here and get one diaper and the wipes. Why are you trying to carry all of that, Sage?"

"I was trying to bring a lot so Justice wouldn't have to come back upstairs. Sorry for cursing, it slipped."

"Well, don't let it slip again. Cursing is something you won't be doing anymore. Is that understood?"

"Yes. I'm sorry," he sniffled.

"You don't have anything to cry about, Sage," I said, placing Faith on the changing table. "Come here." Wrapping my arm around his shoulder while holding Faith's leg, I looked down at him. "Clean your face. It's not okay to curse, but now that we know it's wrong, it won't happen again, right"

"It won't happen again," Sage said, wiping at his eyes.

"Good. Now be a big boy and pick out a sleeper for your sister."

Sage and I together to get Faith cleaned up and I loved how mature he was for his age. Bria was all he had and it showed that he was only around kids at school. He was older than his years but there was still time to allow him to be a kid. I didn't realize how long I was upstairs until we were heading downstairs. Donovan's voice echoed off the walls.

"You're going to love it, Bria! There's more than enough space for all your business supplies and we will even buy anything else you would like to add. The only thing left to do is get you moved from Detroit and back here."

"Uncle Donovan!" Sage said, stumbling down the stairs. I was glad he was holding on to the banister and that's what saved his ass.

"Sage, you're going to break your neck! Slow down," I said in a shaky voice.

"Hey lil man," Wes said, appearing at the bottom of the stairs.

"Uncle Wes!"

"What did you call me?"

"Umm, I called you Uncle Wes, but I meant Dad. You know I'm just learning so it's gonna take some time. Cut a kid some slack!" Sage said, reaching up for a hug.

"You got it," Wes laughed. "What you been up to?"

"I helped change Faith. You missed it; she was stinky."

"That's every day. I didn't miss nothing. Hey, sis."

"Hey, Wes," I said as I leaned in to give him a quick hug.

"Hello! You didn't say anything to my sister! She needs love too!"

Wes started laughing as he swooped Sage into his arm and reached for Faith. Watching him cuddle both of his kids was a sight to see and I couldn't wait to see Donovan as a father to our child.

We entered the living room and Donovan was sitting across from Bria and Juice with a mug on his face. I knew when I was coming down the stairs, I heard him saying Bria would love what I assumed was a house. That must've been the business they had to handle.

"You mean to tell me you're now considering not moving here *after* I just bought you a whole crib? You don't even know this nigga to be talking about moving to California with him! Juice is my nigga, but get to know him first before making a drastic decision like that, Bria. I would hate for you to move and this nigga do you dirty and I have to kill him."

"Dap, you know I'm not that type of nigga. I understand what you're saying and I respect it. I've known your sister for a short time, but I've learned a lot about her in that period as well. There's no certain timeframe to love anyone and I'm feeling her, bro." Juice looked over at Bria and tweaked her nose with his finger and she smiled.

"Hearing Bria say she wanted to move to Cali was a surprise to me. I agree with you about that part," Juice addressed Dap. "There are some things I have to get in place before that can happen, but I'm willing to come here often until the time is right for us to make that move. In the meantime, enjoy the crib, Bria. We have a lifetime to spend together."

I walked over and sat on Donovan's lap and kissed his lips softly. "Hey baby. What's going on?" I asked.

"I'll explain later."

Wes Sr. sat up on the couch with his legs slightly parted. "Jamal, I appreciate you coming over to help care for Bria, but I don't think her moving is a good idea at this moment."

"Daddy, I've been on my own for almost six years without anyone except Sage. I haven't been in any relationship and now that someone has come in my life, I'm getting major backlash for wanting to pursue something for myself." Bria finally spoke up for herself.

"Bria, I don't think they are lashing out to stop what you're trying to accomplish. All they want is for you to get to know Juice better. If you move and things don't work out, it will bring a lot of friction between Donovan and his friend. Make sure the foundation is solid before making a drastic move by moving across the country. Juice is seeing things in the same aspect. Sometimes distance makes a relationship grow into something far better."

I didn't want to say anything, but hearing my take on the situation might allow Bria to see things from a woman's perspective. Justice nodded her head in agreement and Bria saw it too. The room became quiet but as usual, Sage broke the ice.

"Mommy Bria, I want you to stay here with me until I get used to living with Daddy Wes and Justice. Maybe after I'm comfortable, you can move with Juice Man. I know you like him a lot because I caught y'all kissing," he giggled.

"You are one nosy little boy. Wes, when are you packing him up to live here forever?" Bria asked playfully.

"Soon as I get the keys to our new home and get moved out of here," Wes said, turning to Justice. "Yeah, baby. I purchased us a new place and wanted it to be a surprise, but since we're on the subject of people moving, I decided to let the cat out of the bag. We are almost over the shit that's been going on and I want to start over fresh."

"You bought me a house, Wes! Oh my God, thank you. baby!" Justice said kissing him passionately.

Wes cut his eyes at Donovan and I had a feeling there was a hidden message in there somewhere. I was glad Wes thought to move my friend out of this house because after what happened, I didn't deem the place safe. They needed to move because Shanell knew where they lived.

"Bria and Juice, take things slow and if it was meant to be it would be. There's no reason to rush into a relationship. Let's eat. I know everyone is hungry," Justice said walking to the kitchen. "In the words of Beverly, wash ya hands before you sit at my damn table."

Everyone laughed and scrambled up to wash up so they could eat.

Chapter 25

Lucci

Arturro was dead and I still couldn't believe it. Dap had crossed the line when he had a gift-wrapped package delivered to the front desk of the hotel I was staying in with Shanell. Inside was Arturro's pinky finger with the diamond ring I'd bought him for his birthday last year. The shit crushed my heart, but I knew coming for Dap would have problems that came along with it.

The bitch Shanell was vicious and a muthafuckin' thief. She stole money from me and didn't even lie about doing the shit. I should've taken heed to what Dap told me over the phone, but I didn't think she was that damn bad. After the package was delivered, I wasted no time checking out of the hotel. They had to be watching our every move, so I had to convince Shanell to leave her car along with my rental in the hotel parking lot. We had to make Dap and his people think we were just hiding out in the hotel.

I requested an Uber, went to the hotel that Kalene was staying in, and banged on the door. She opened the door with a scowl on her face and I could tell she was high as fuck. Her hair was all over her head and her body odor was foul.

"Kalene, what the fuck is wrong with you? Your habit is what fucked shit up with you getting close to that nigga Dap!" I screamed, pushing my way into the room with Shanell behind me.

We had all of our bags in tow and I knew it was going to be a problem. Me and Kalene had been fucking around and it was the reason she left Dap. I sold her ass a dream and she fell for it. Kalene fell in love with the thought of being a billionaire's wife and the thing she got out of it was designer clothes and a coke habit she couldn't control.

"Wait a minute, Lucci! What the fuck is this bitch doing here? Is this who you've been with all this time?"

"Call me another bitch and I'll cut yo' muthafuckin' tongue out yo' mouth. Move outta of my way, because we're about to be roommates until we get at this nigga Dap. You are the only bitch he ain't giving no attention to."

Shanell had a way with words and her attitude was dangerous as fuck. The last thing I needed was Kalene getting into some shit with her that she wouldn't be able to get out of. Standing between the two of them, I held my hands up and turned to Shanell to calm her down.

"Look, Shanell. All of that is not necessary. We need Kalene because we have nowhere else to go."

"Nah, you need her! I can go find a hole in the wall motel to shack up in. But you better tell her to watch her mouth when addressing me. I don't do well with disrespect and you know this firsthand. How the fuck was you with a bitch that's on that shit?"

"Was? He's still with me! He's only fucking you to get at Dap! Get that shit right!"

"Both of y'all shut up! Kalene, we just need to crash with you for a minute. When we leave to go back to Cali, you know what it is."

"See, bitch, I told you," Kalene said, hugging me around my neck.

I didn't think Shanell gave a damn because she walked deeper into the room, set her bags in the corner, and sat down in a chair. Kalene kissed my lips and my dick grew in my pants. I was surprised because Shanell had milked my ass dry and I didn't think it would work anymore. Pulling back, I propped my luggage against the wall and went into the bathroom to drain the weasel.

"Bitch, you need to leave that shit alone so you can have a level head with all the shit that's going on around you. Let me ask you this, how the fuck you leave a nigga like Dap for Lucci? That nigga is traveling with all the money to his name in a suitcase." Shanell laughed.

I didn't find that shit funny at all as I shook my dick and flushed the toilet. I waited to see what Kalene would say because I swore to myself that I would slap the shit out of her if she said something stupid. Opting not to wash my hands, I exited the bathroom and Kalene's head was lowered to sniff the lines on a mirror. Her head shot back and she held her nose with her left hand as she sniffed loudly.

"Lay off that shit, Kalene!" I barked, rushing over snatching the mirror from her.

"I need that, Lucci! There was a point when you would be partying with me," Kalene screamed, trying to get the coke back. "You may need to do a line of two yourself. Maybe it would calm your ass down from talking to me reckless around this bitch!" My eyes shot to Shanell and I saw her face contort, but I wasn't going to let her do anything to Kalene.

"Here, snort all that shit if you want to. I have moves to make and I don't have time to listen to this back and forth between y'all. Play nice until I come back."

"I'm going with you because I can't promise she'll still be breathing when you return," Shanell said, standing to her feet.

"You're not coming with me. Leave if you want, but I have something to do on my own."

I left before Shanell could utter another word. Talking to her was like talking to a brick wall. It wasn't worth it.

Walking out into the cool Chicago air, I pulled my phone from my pocket and hit up my uncle Christian.

"Ciao."

"Zio Christian, sono Lucci. Ho bisogno di verderti. Arturro é morto. Sei ancora a Chicago?" (Uncle Christian, it's Lucci. I need to see you. Arturro is dead. Are you still Chicago?)

"What do you mean Arturro is dead? Where are you?"

"I don't want to disclose my location over the phone. Meet me at that Grant Park place. There's a big fountain in the middle of the park. It's not on. We should be able to talk privately. I'm on my way there now, see you soon."

The park was down the street and took no time for me to get there. My brother's voice echoed in my head and I shook it away. If it wasn't for me, he'd still be alive and I felt bad about that shit. Dap wasn't playing fair with his get back and I didn't know which way he would come next. He had already killed everybody that I came to Chicago with and I had no one to run to except my uncle.

Christian was affiliated with Dap, but I didn't think he thought me and Arturro had anything to do with my father's death because he hadn't treated us any differently. I needed him to help me get the insurance money and to get Customs from Dap.

There wasn't anyone outside and I was walking down the street checking my surroundings. My nerves were on edge because I didn't know if someone would appear and take me out. I won't lie, I was scared as hell. As I entered the park, I made my way to the fountain and sat on the edge of the ledge. I tried hard to picture how the water looked when the fountain was on, but nothing came to mind.

"Lucci."

I heard Christian's voice and stood quickly. "Uncle Christian. I'm so glad to see you. They killed my brother and every-one that came to Chicago with me."

"Who is they?"

"Dap and whoever's helping him. Probably Juice and Kato! Hell, I don't know!"

"What reason did Dap have for killing Arturro? I know damn well it had nothing to do with the fight from the club. You got your ass whooped and I told you to go back to California and leave that alone."

"That had to be the reason. There was no other reason," I lied as I held my head down.

"Lucci, I've been your uncle all your life. I know when you're lying. What did you do?"

Turning away from my uncle, I thought long and hard if I wanted to tell him the truth or continue to lie. Bad as I wanted to lie, I couldn't come up with one that was going to be believable enough. I glanced up at my uncle and took a deep breath as I collected my thoughts.

"You know how I felt about my dad passing his company down to Dap. All I wanted was for him to give me back what is rightfully mine. Customs belongs to me!"

190

"No, Customs doesn't belong to you, Lucci. Rocco molded the person he wanted to take over something he worked hard to build from the ground. Dap just so happened to be that person."

"Why would he look over his own sons? That shit was wrong and you know it!" I was pissed and I was yelling, something I'd never done to my uncle. The respect was high when it came to Christian but he was justifying the bullshit.

"You're not going to raise your voice at me, Lucci. On second thought, go ahead and let everything out. This is your chance to speak your mind. Anything goes. You have the floor."

"Answer the question. Why did he look me and my brother over for someone that's not family?" I asked.

"Luciano, you and Arturro weren't mature enough to run Rocco's Jewels. Every time he tried to teach the two of you the business, the streets were where y'all wanted to be. I don't think he would've care if his sons were making their own money any way possible. But that's not what was going on. You made money by constantly going to your father to provide."

"That was his job! It's not like he didn't have the money to give. Why did we have to work, when our father had money falling out his ass? We didn't have to work!" I yelled.

"And that's the reason Dap was the chosen one! He proved to my brother that his business wouldn't get run into the ground without him standing over him to make it happen. Dap took what he was taught and made it work for him. In turn, he turned your father's business into something that would prosper for years to come. I'm not going to sit here and go back and forth with you, Lucci. Tell me why Dap would have a reason to kill Arturro!"

"I sent Franco and Piero to kidnap his brother's wife. I wanted him to know that I wasn't playing games about my money!"

"In turn, you got your brother killed for something you have no rights to. That was stupid!"

"Don't call me stupid! That's the reason your brother is six feet under now. He called me stupid one too many times." I regretted letting the words come out of my mouth. Christian stood stoned faced but I knew the wheels were turning in his head.

"Lucci, did you just insinuate that you killed my brother?" he asked.

"I didn't insinuate anything." I had already said the shit, so there was no use backtracking my statement. "I killed his ass because he refused to give me and Arturro any more money. Knowing we were in his will as the beneficiaries, I came up with a plan to kill him. I was going to get the money that was rightfully mine one way or the other."

Christian stood with his hands behind his back and I could see the hurt in his eyes. It meant nothing to me because he knew about my father's plans before they became a reality. He should've talked him out of doing what he did and he didn't, so he was partially to blame too.

"Lucci, you killed your father for something you're not even going to receive. My brother took you and your brother off of his policy as beneficiaries almost a year before you took his life. He knew that the two of you were not going to do right by his money. Again, he worked hard for his money and that's all the two of you wanted him for. Every damn day he was treated like a fuckin' money cow! I'm ashamed to call you my family."

Christian had tears running down his face but I had no remorse for him. Just like I thought, he knew! The things he revealed made me wish I had brought my gun with me. My uncle would've died that night.

"The amount of money you and Arturro were going to receive was one hundred thousand dollars. What you weren't supposed to know was that Dap is the beneficiary of his estate. See Lucci, you lost to Dap once again. He is a billionaire and you ain't shit. You killed my brother, your father because you are one greedy bastard! You don't have to worry about Dap coming for you. I waited months for you to put your foot in your mouth and admit to killing my only brother. I knew the day Arturro died, and now you will join him."

Christian's arm came from behind his back as he finished what he was saying and I knew I was going to die. There was nothing I could do because my feet felt as if they were glued to the ground. I said a silent prayer, but before I could get past "Lord, please forgive me", a bullet pierced my skull and life as I knew it was gone forever.

Meesha

Chapter 26

Shanell

Lucci hadn't return from wherever he went last night. I ended up going to sleep in the chair because I sat watching Kalene snort coke until damn near two in the morning.

It was six o'clock and I had to piss like a race horse. Racing to the bathroom, I relieved my bladder and thought about what my next move would be. There was no way I was going to sit in the hotel room until Lucci returned.

After washing my hands, I went back out into the room for my bag to get an outfit out for the day. The room was quiet and the hairs stood up on my neck. Something wasn't right, there was an eerie feeling in the air. I stopped what I was doing and turned around. Kalene was still in the same position she was in when I woke up briefly around four in the morning.

I crept over to the bed and I was scared to even move the covers back away from her face. The way her hand was positioned, I knew she was gone. I just wanted to see for myself if she was dead or not. When I pulled the covers back, Kalene's face was a grayish color and her lips were blue. I was mad as hell because I didn't get the chance to off her ass myself.

That was my cue to get out of Dodge. I didn't bother washing my ass. Stuffing my belongings back into my bag, I rushed to the door and hit my leg on something hard. I looked down and noticed Lucci's luggage. Remembering the money, I searched through it and transferred every dollar to my bag. I glanced over my shoulder at Kalene one more time before opening the door.

There was no one in the hallway, so I beelined to the stairwell. In my heart, I knew Lucci was dead. I called his phone numerous times last night to no avail. He knew I was seconds away from smacking the hell out of Kalene before he left, so he would've answered to make sure I didn't kill her.

Without being seen by anyone in the hotel, I made my way to one of the back exits and walked down Michigan Avenue until I could hail a cab back to the Radisson to get my car. What were the chances Dap still had someone watching it knowing I hadn't been out in days? At that time, I was going to take my chances because I had to get out of the city.

Flagging down a cab, I jumped in the back and gave the driver my destination. It took about five minutes to get there, but I had him to drive around the corner before I got out after paying the fare. Walking swiftly to the back parking lot behind the hotel, I hit the fob on my keys, jumped in the driver's seat, and started the car immediately. As I waited for the engine to warm up, I thought about Sage.

I wanted to change my life and wanted to be a mother to the child I gave life to. The things I did through the years and in the past few months were wrong, but it was time for me to leave and start over. There was no way I could do that without including my son. Pulling my phone from my purse, I took a huge risk of reaching out to Sage. I used my iCloud email to Facetime him on his tablet.

Sage's face appeared on the screen and I smiled. "Hello, Sage," I said happily. Sage looked behind him and I had a feeling he was going to call out to someone and reveal I reached out to him. "Don't tell anyone I'm talking to you, Sage. Please."

"Auntie Nell, I won't tell anyone. Where are you?"

"I can't tell you that right now, baby. I want to see you. Tell me where you are."

"I'm at my daddy's house. Why didn't you tell me Wes was my daddy?"

"Sage, I tried to tell you I was your mommy and you didn't believe me. If I had told you Wes was your father, you would've wanted to see him."

"I've always wanted a father, Auntie Nell. You did a lot of bad things. I don't want to see you. Leave us alone. I have to go before daddy comes back. I'm not supposed to be on my tablet and I was told to be a big boy and don't answer the door for anybody. Don't come here, Auntie Nell."

Sage hung up before I could say anything further and that pissed me off. Throwing the car in drive, I backed out of the spot and sped onto the main street. I couldn't go on in this life without my son. He was going wherever I ended up because I'm his mother.

"Wes and that bitch will not raise my son!" I screamed out as I headed toward Wes' home.

The street was quiet being that it was barely eight in the morning. I parked down the street and walked back to Wes' home. Peering through the kitchen window, I didn't see any movement inside. I stomped through the flowerbed and looked through another window and there sat Sage. He was sitting on the floor watching TV.

I stood admiring him for at least thirty minutes and no one came in to check on him. At first, I thought he was lying about being home alone. Now I knew he actually told the truth and it was the perfect time for me to get him out of the house. I tapped on the window and Sage's head swiveled around and I waved wildly at him.

Sage stood up and came to the window. There was something in his eyes that I couldn't put my finger on, but I didn't think much about it. I needed to convince Sage to open the door for me. Pointing my finger toward the front door, I said loudly, "Open the door."

"I can't! I'm going to get in trouble, Auntie Nell."

"You won't. I'm going to the door. Open it for me, Sage."

I left the window and stood in front of the door and waited for it to open. After a few minutes, I turned the knob and the door was still locked. Knocking hard, I finally heard his little feet coming to let me in. When the lock was released, I entered the home of Wes and his wife and the alarm beeped.

"Damn I didn't think about the alarm being on," I said under my breath. I had fifteen seconds before the police would be summoned to the residence so I had to think fast. Remembering the night I drugged Wes, I closed my eyes and the code popped in my head with five seconds to spare. "5170. Please let him be the stupid one to still have the same code." The alarm disarmed and I slammed the door turning to Sage.

"I told you not to come," he said, backing away from me.

Sage's eyes shifted upward and I was hit upside the head from behind. I fell face first onto the floor and all I remembered was Sage falling backwards and crying.

***

My head was banging and I couldn't move my arms. The weight of my body felt as if it was expended in the air. Struggling to open my eyes, I was finally able to pry them open a little but everything was blurry. I blinked a couple times and my sight started adjusting to the dimly lit room.

"Glad to see you finally decided to wake up. How's your head?" Justice appeared in the doorway with a sly smile on her face. "A hard head makes a soft ass, Shanell. Didn't I tell you to stay the fuck away from my family?"

"Bitch, fuck you!" I snarled, realizing my hands were chained and I was hanging from a ceiling. Turning my head from side to side, I couldn't tell where I was, but it was definitely going to be the place I'd be when I took my last breath. "Let me down and we can fight heads up!"

"I'm not fighting yo' ass anymore. For what? I've beat yo' ass already. We're going to try something different this time around," she laughed.

Justice strolled into the room with a metal bat in her hand. Coward ass bitch was about to fuck me up and there was no way for me to defend myself. Oh well, I guess it was time for me to talk my shit until she took me out.

"What, you mad because I fucked yo' husband?" I laughed. "Bitch, you ain't shit! Wes is going to find another bitch and cheat again. Getting rid of me ain't gon' solve your problem, wifey."

"Nah, I'm not mad. Far from it. See, what you don't understand is that you violated in too many ways. You thought you were going to continue to hurt, kill, and destroy people. You thought wrong!"

Justice swung the bat and hit me in my ribs. Excruciating pain shot through my body as I heard my bones shatter. My breath caught in my throat and I struggled to breathe.

"Aaaaaah!" I screamed out in pain. Every breath I sucked in hurt like a muthafucka. "That's all you got? Try it again but this time, step in a little more and follow through with your swing."

Justice switch the bat to the left side and swung again. She hit my left leg like she was swinging at a piñata. My leg was dangling and my bones felt like they fell to my foot. The pain was indescribable, but I refused to show how much pain I was in. Instead, I gritted my teeth and fought to get my wrist loose.

"That's enough, Justice. Let her ass hang there for a minute," Wes said as he entered.

"Hey, baby daddy," I choked out. "You know everything happened because I love you. All you had to do was love me back."

"Shanell, that's not how you love anybody. You killed my muthafuckin' mama! Why?"

"Why did I kill Beverly? Well, Wes, your mother should've never tried to jump bad with her old ass. All she had to do was shut the fuck up and die quietly. She wasn't going to talk her way out of that death."

I laughed through the pain, but I saw the anger on Wes' face. He stepped forward just as Dap, Wes Sr., and a few other niggas walked into the room. Everybody came to see my ass die.

"Don't waste your time putting your hands on this bitch, bro. Fuck her. We'll see her ass in the afterlife one day. Until then, we'll let our little friends have their way with her. Clear the room," Dap said, leaving out as everyone followed.

Justice was the last one to exit and I hocked up a mouthful of spit and shot it in her direction. She smiled and let the door close behind her. There was a sound that filled the room and the walls dropped, revealing everyone that had left a few minutes prior. I had no clue what they had in store for me, but I kind of knew it wasn't going to be good for me.

"Shanell, I hope my friends aren't too hard on you." Wes' voice filled the room.

My body felt as if it was on fire and I just wanted all the pain to go away. A small door opened on the wall and I heard a loud growl followed by the chains that held my wrists starting to move upward.

A fuckin' tiger came out of the hole and I kicked my right leg as I fought to get out of the chains. Being raised toward the ceiling was good for me, but I knew I wasn't going to remain in that position. These muthafuckas brought animals for little ole me. They could've shot my ass and been done with it.

There were a total of four tigers walking around the room and it seemed as if they were sniffing the air, trying to find their prey. The chains started moving downward and I couldn't believe they were going to feed me to these cats! I started screaming, hoping someone would hear me on the outside.

"Please, Wes, I'm sorry! I don't want to die like this!"

"My mama didn't get a courtesy saving either. It's not about to end well for you, Nell. Adios, bitch!"

I was dropped to the floor and the tigers wasted no time charging at me full speed. The first one grabbed my left foot in its mouth, but the nerves in it were dead. I couldn't feel anything. My arm was ripped from my body and I couldn't make a sound. I blacked out and my spirit floated and I was finally free from all the bullshit I had conjured up on Earth.

Epilogue

Six months later

Dap

Witnessing Shanell get ripped limb from limb by those tigers was the best thing I'd ever witnessed in my life. As gruesome as it was, she deserved everything that happened to her. Will I burn in hell for enjoying the moment and making it happen? Yep, maybe I would later down the line but for now, I was enjoying the birth of my first child.

Life had been great between Tana and myself and I'd waited on this day since the doctors informed me that she was pregnant. Being in the delivery room opened up sweat glands I never knew I had. A nigga was sweating bullets with every contraction Tana experienced.

"You're never getting any more pussy! I'm not going through this pain again in life!" Tana screamed after the contraction went away. The last time the nurse checked her, she was seven centimeters and they had been easing along slowly for the past five hours.

"Baby, you don't mean that. The pain will be over soon and you'll be right back to lovin' me." I leaned in to give her a kiss on her lips and she pushed my face away.

"Oh my God! These things are coming closer together, Dap! Get this baby out of me now!"

Pushing the button for the nurse, she didn't respond but instead came right to the room. "Is everything alright, Miss Taylor?"

"No, I feel like this baby is coming. It's at the opening and it burns," Tana cried.

"You were only seven centimeters last time I checked," the nurse said, pulling on a pair of gloves. "Let's see what's going on here." She checked Tana's cervix and immediately ran out of the room.

When she returned, she had Dr. Sutcliff in tow and he started getting ready to see what was going on. He checked Tana and smiled. "With the next contraction, I want you to push, Montana. You are correct, the baby is tired of waiting and is ready to make its debut into the world. Dad, are you going to cut the cord?"

"Hell yeah, let's do it!" I said excitedly.

The baby monitor sounded and I knew another contraction was coming and all Tana had to do was push. Grasping her hand, I stood by her side and she squeezed tightly as the nurse pushed both of her legs back to her chest. She started trying to do the breathing techniques she had learned in Lamaze class, but all that shit went out the window.

"On the count of three, I want you to push until I count to ten. One. Two. Three! Push, Montana!" the doctor said as he started counting. "I see the head. Stop pushing. Let's do it again on the count of three. One. Two. Three!"

Tana was sweating and grunting as she pushed her heart out. I grabbed a couple napkins from the nightstand, wiping her face while she damn near broke my fingers. I peered over Tana's legs and I could see the top of my seed's head. Tears stung my eyes, but I was too tough to be in this bitch crying.

"Give me one more push and it's going to be the little one's birthday." Dr. Sutcliff explained.

"I'm too tired. I don't think I can go on," Tana said tiredly.

"You can and you will. One more push, baby, you got this." I kissed the top of her head and moved her hair off her forehead.

Tana took a deep breath and pushed with all her might when she was given the green light. "Fuck!"

I pried my hand from Tana's and made my way to the end of the bed to see what was going on. My baby was in the palm of Dr. Sutcliff's hand and he was rubbing it on the back as the nurse suctioned all the guck out of its mouth. One long wipe and a loud wail filled the room. I let out the air I'd been holding from the moment my baby was born and no sound was heard.

"We have a boy! Congratulations! Do the honors, dad," Dr. Sutcliff said handing me the scissors to cut the umbilical cord.

Once the cord was cut, the nurse rushed the baby to the other side of the room and cleaned my seed up. Tana laid on the bed with her eyes closed. My baby was tired and she did a great job delivery our child.

"I love you, Montana King," I whispered in her ear. Her response was a series of snores and I couldn't do nothing but laugh because she earned that shit. Kissing her on the lips, I went over to the baby bed to check on my junior while his mama rested up.

"He's eight pounds, thirteen ounces, and twenty inches long," the nurse said over my baby's cries. "Do you have a name for him?"

"Of course, I do. He will be Donovan Latrell King Jr." My son looked just like me and I was proud as hell and couldn't wait to show him off. Snapping a couple pictures, I sent them in a group text and told everyone to come to the hospital. It was time for me to do what I had been holding out on for this moment.

Tana woke up about an hour later and I was sitting with DJ cradled in my arms. Standing to my feet, I placed him on her chest as the door opened. All of our family and my niggas from Cali filled the room with gifts and balloons. Congratulations were given as well as hugs.

"I asked everyone here to meet my son, Donovan Latrell King Jr. There's no way my seed will exist in this world and his mother don't share the same last name he has." I turned to Tana and smiled. "With that being said, Montana Taylor, will you make my day and agree to be my wife? Without you, there's no me and I want you to have my last name, ma."

"Awwwww, Donovan! Yes, I will be honored to be your wife!"

The room filled with claps, whistles, and hoots from everyone in attendance. I kissed my future wife deeply and kissed my son on the top of his head before excusing myself to use the bathroom. While standing at the sink, I reflected on everything we'd been through in the past ten months and I cried for every moment.

My life was finally on the right track. Customs was back up and running better than ever. I had opened King's Apparel and it was striving just as strong as Customs. I made sure my pops would be straight for the rest of his life by giving him three million dollars. At first, he turned it down, but I didn't let him convince me to take it back. Life without Beverly was getting better for him. The grand-kids kept him pretty busy.

Wes and Justice moved into their new home. Sage was adjusting very well to his new surroundings and he was loving the school he attended. Faith had started walking and was now terrorizing everything and everyone around her. Justice went back to work, showcased her talents, and earned a huge promotion. Wes quit his job at Citywide and opened up his own architectural company. King's Architect was on its way to the top.

Bria moved into the home I bought for her and healed completely from her injuries. Her online business was booming and my sister was happy again. Juice was right by her side whenever he came to visit. He was getting his shit in order for when he came to claim his woman permanently.

The day we killed Shanell was the same day I found out Kalene died of an overdose. I was sad that she got caught up in the lifestyle of drugs. I didn't hate her. Tana filled in the hole that was created when Kalene left me. I had all the love I needed, but I still had a spot in my heart for Kalene.

I contacted her family and passed on the news I'd learned. I paid for her body to be returned to California and also for her funeral service. It was the least I could do. But now that I had my own family, I could take this Daddy shit to another level.

People are brought in your life for many reasons. Some to learn lessons from, others to help you along the way, and others to make you realize how strong you really are. I've had people to fill all of those categorize, and I don't regret anything that I've had to go through to weed out the bad seeds. Keep your eyes open so you can do the same.

The End

Submission Guideline

Submit the first three chapters of your completed manuscript to ldpsubmissions@gmail.com, subject line: Your book's title. The manuscript must be in a .doc file and sent as an attachment. Document should be in Times New Roman, double spaced and in size 12 font. Also, provide your synopsis and full contact information. If sending multiple submissions, they must each be in a separate email.

Have a story but no way to send it electronically? You can still submit to LDP/Ca$h Presents. Send in the first three chapters, written or typed, of your completed manuscript to:

LDP: Submissions Dept
Po Box 944
Stockbridge, Ga 30281

DO NOT send original manuscript. Must be a duplicate.

Provide your synopsis and a cover letter containing your full contact information.

Thanks for considering LDP and Ca$h Presents.

<u>Coming Soon from Lock Down Publications/Ca\$h Presents</u>

BOW DOWN TO MY GANGSTA

By **Ca\$h**

TORN BETWEEN TWO

By **Coffee**

THE STREETS STAINED MY SOUL **II**

By **Marcellus Allen**

BLOOD OF A BOSS **VI**

SHADOWS OF THE GAME II

By **Askari**

LOYAL TO THE GAME **IV**

By **T.J. & Jelissa**

A DOPEBOY'S PRAYER **II**

By **Eddie "Wolf" Lee**

IF LOVING YOU IS WRONG… **III**

By **Jelissa**

TRUE SAVAGE **VII**

MIDNIGHT CARTEL III

DOPE BOY MAGIC IV

By **Chris Green**

BLAST FOR ME **III**

A SAVAGE DOPEBOY III

CUTTHROAT MAFIA II

By **Ghost**

A HUSTLER'S DECEIT III

KILL ZONE **II**

BAE BELONGS TO ME III

A DOPE BOY'S QUEEN II

By **Aryanna**

CHAINED TO THE STREETS III

By **J-Blunt**

KING OF NEW YORK V

COKE KINGS IV

By **T.J. Edwards**

GORILLAZ IN THE BAY V

TEARS OF A GANGSTA II

De'Kari

THE STREETS ARE CALLING II

Duquie Wilson

KINGPIN KILLAZ IV

STREET KINGS III

PAID IN BLOOD III

CARTEL KILLAZ IV

DOPE GODS II

Hood Rich

SINS OF A HUSTLA II

ASAD

TRIGGADALE III

Elijah R. Freeman

KINGZ OF THE GAME V

Playa Ray

SLAUGHTER GANG IV

RUTHLESS HEART IV

By Willie Slaughter

THE HEART OF A SAVAGE III

By Jibril Williams

FUK SHYT II

By Blakk Diamond

THE DOPEMAN'S BODYGAURD II

Meesha

By Tranay Adams

TRAP GOD II

By Troublesome

YAYO III

A SHOOTER'S AMBITION III

By S. Allen

GHOST MOB

Stilloan Robinson

KINGPIN DREAMS II

By Paper Boi Rari

CREAM

By Yolanda Moore

SON OF A DOPE FIEND II

By Renta

FOREVER GANGSTA II

GLOCKS ON SATIN SHEETS II

By Adrian Dulan

LOYALTY AIN'T PROMISED II

By Keith Williams

THE PRICE YOU PAY FOR LOVE II

DOPE GIRL MAGIC II

By Destiny Skai

TOE TAGZ III

By Ah'Million

CONFESSIONS OF A GANGSTA II

By Nicholas Lock

I'M NOTHING WITHOUT HIS LOVE II

By Monet Dragun

CAUGHT UP IN THE LIFE II

By Robert Baptiste

208

NEW TO THE GAME III

By **Malik D. Rice**

LIFE OF A SAVAGE III

By **Romell Tukes**

QUIET MONEY II

By **Trai'Quan**

THE STREETS MADE ME II

By **Larry D. Wright**

THE ULTIMATE SACRIFICE VI

By **Anthony Fields**

THE LIFE OF A HOOD STAR

By Ca$h & Rashia Wilson

<u>Available Now</u>

RESTRAINING ORDER **I & II**

By **CA$H & Coffee**

LOVE KNOWS NO BOUNDARIES **I II & III**

By **Coffee**

RAISED AS A GOON I, II, III & IV

BRED BY THE SLUMS I, II, III

BLAST FOR ME I & II

ROTTEN TO THE CORE I II III

A BRONX TALE I, II, III

DUFFEL BAG CARTEL I II III IV

HEARTLESS GOON I II III IV

A SAVAGE DOPEBOY I II

HEARTLESS GOON I II III

DRUG LORDS I II III

CUTTHROAT MAFIA

By **Ghost**

LAY IT DOWN **I & II**

LAST OF A DYING BREED

BLOOD STAINS OF A SHOTTA I & II III

By **Jamaica**

LOYAL TO THE GAME I II III

LIFE OF SIN I, II III

By **TJ & Jelissa**

BLOODY COMMAS I & II

SKI MASK CARTEL I II & III

KING OF NEW YORK I II,III IV

RISE TO POWER I II III

COKE KINGS I II III

BORN HEARTLESS I II III IV

By **T.J. Edwards**

IF LOVING HIM IS WRONG...I & II

LOVE ME EVEN WHEN IT HURTS I II III

By **Jelissa**

WHEN THE STREETS CLAP BACK I & II III

THE HEART OF A SAVAGE I II

By **Jibril Williams**

A DISTINGUISHED THUG STOLE MY HEART I II & III

LOVE SHOULDN'T HURT I II III IV

RENEGADE BOYS I II III IV

PAID IN KARMA I II III

By **Meesha**

A GANGSTER'S CODE I &, II III

A GANGSTER'S SYN I II III

THE SAVAGE LIFE I II III

CHAINED TO THE STREETS I II

By J-Blunt

PUSH IT TO THE LIMIT

By **Bre' Hayes**

BLOOD OF A BOSS **I, II, III, IV, V**

SHADOWS OF THE GAME

By **Askari**

THE STREETS BLEED MURDER **I, II & III**

THE HEART OF A GANGSTA I II& III

By **Jerry Jackson**

CUM FOR ME I II III IV V

An **LDP Erotica Collaboration**

BRIDE OF A HUSTLA **I II & II**

THE FETTI GIRLS **I, II& III**

CORRUPTED BY A GANGSTA I, II III, IV

BLINDED BY HIS LOVE

THE PRICE YOU PAY FOR LOVE

DOPE GIRL MAGIC

By **Destiny Skai**

WHEN A GOOD GIRL GOES BAD

By **Adrienne**

THE COST OF LOYALTY I II III

By Kweli

A GANGSTER'S REVENGE **I II III & IV**

THE BOSS MAN'S DAUGHTERS I II III IV V

A SAVAGE LOVE **I & II**

BAE BELONGS TO ME I II

A HUSTLER'S DECEIT I, II, III

WHAT BAD BITCHES DO I, II, III

SOUL OF A MONSTER I II III

KILL ZONE

A DOPE BOY'S QUEEN

By **Aryanna**

A KINGPIN'S AMBITON

A KINGPIN'S AMBITION **II**

I MURDER FOR THE DOUGH

By **Ambitious**

TRUE SAVAGE I II III IV V VI

DOPE BOY MAGIC I, II, III

MIDNIGHT CARTEL I II

By **Chris Green**

A DOPEBOY'S PRAYER

By **Eddie "Wolf" Lee**

THE KING CARTEL **I, II & III**

By **Frank Gresham**

THESE NIGGAS AIN'T LOYAL **I, II & III**

By **Nikki Tee**

GANGSTA SHYT **I II &III**

By **CATO**

THE ULTIMATE BETRAYAL

By **Phoenix**

BOSS'N UP **I , II & III**

By **Royal Nicole**

I LOVE YOU TO DEATH

By Destiny J

I RIDE FOR MY HITTA

I STILL RIDE FOR MY HITTA

By **Misty Holt**

LOVE & CHASIN' PAPER

By **Qay Crockett**
TO DIE IN VAIN
SINS OF A HUSTLA
By **ASAD**
BROOKLYN HUSTLAZ
By **Boogsy Morina**
BROOKLYN ON LOCK I & II
By **Sonovia**
GANGSTA CITY
By **Teddy Duke**
A DRUG KING AND HIS DIAMOND I & II III
A DOPEMAN'S RICHES
HER MAN, MINE'S TOO I, II
CASH MONEY HO'S
By Nicole Goosby
TRAPHOUSE KING **I II & III**
KINGPIN KILLAZ I II III
STREET KINGS I II
PAID IN BLOOD **I II**
CARTEL KILLAZ I II III
DOPE GODS
By **Hood Rich**
LIPSTICK KILLAH **I, II, III**
CRIME OF PASSION I II & III
By **Mimi**
STEADY MOBBN' **I, II, III**
THE STREETS STAINED MY SOUL
By **Marcellus Allen**
WHO SHOT YA **I, II, III**
SON OF A DOPE FIEND

Renta

GORILLAZ IN THE BAY **I II III IV**

TEARS OF A GANGSTA

DE'KARI

TRIGGADALE I II

Elijah R. Freeman

GOD BLESS THE TRAPPERS I, II, III

THESE SCANDALOUS STREETS I, II, III

FEAR MY GANGSTA I, II, III

THESE STREETS DON'T LOVE NOBODY I, II

BURY ME A G I, II, III, IV, V

A GANGSTA'S EMPIRE I, II, III, IV

THE DOPEMAN'S BODYGAURD

Tranay Adams

THE STREETS ARE CALLING

Duquie Wilson

MARRIED TO A BOSS... I II III

By Destiny Skai & Chris Green

KINGZ OF THE GAME I II III IV

Playa Ray

SLAUGHTER GANG I II III

RUTHLESS HEART I II III

By Willie Slaughter

FUK SHYT

By Blakk Diamond

DON'T F#CK WITH MY HEART I II

By Linnea

ADDICTED TO THE DRAMA I II III

By Jamila

YAYO I II

A SHOOTER'S AMBITION I II

By S. Allen

TRAP GOD

By Troublesome

FOREVER GANGSTA

GLOCKS ON SATIN SHEETS

By Adrian Dulan

TOE TAGZ I II

By Ah'Million

KINGPIN DREAMS

By Paper Boi Rari

CONFESSIONS OF A GANGSTA

By Nicholas Lock

I'M NOTHING WITHOUT HIS LOVE

By Monet Dragun

CAUGHT UP IN THE LIFE

By Robert Baptiste

NEW TO THE GAME I II

By **Malik D. Rice**

Life of a Savage I II

By **Romell Tukes**

LOYALTY AIN'T PROMISED

By Keith Williams

Quiet Money

By **Trai'Quan**

THE STREETS MADE ME

By **Larry D. Wright**

THE ULTIMATE SACRIFICE I, II, III, IV, V

KHADIFI

By **Anthony Fields**

Meesha

THE LIFE OF A HOOD STAR
By Ca$h & Rashia Wilson

<u>BOOKS BY LDP'S CEO, CA$H</u>

<u>TRUST IN NO MAN</u>
<u>TRUST IN NO MAN 2</u>
<u>TRUST IN NO MAN 3</u>
<u>BONDED BY BLOOD</u>
<u>SHORTY GOT A THUG</u>
<u>THUGS CRY</u>
<u>THUGS CRY 2</u>
<u>THUGS CRY 3</u>
<u>TRUST NO BITCH</u>
<u>TRUST NO BITCH 2</u>
<u>TRUST NO BITCH 3</u>
<u>TIL MY CASKET DROPS</u>
<u>RESTRAINING ORDER</u>
<u>RESTRAINING ORDER 2</u>
<u>IN LOVE WITH A CONVICT</u>
<u>LIFE OF A HOOD STAR</u>

<u>Coming Soon</u>
BONDED BY BLOOD 2
BOW DOWN TO MY GANGSTA

Meesha

Lightning Source UK Ltd.
Milton Keynes UK
UKHW021418030720
365983UK00004B/542

9 781952 936104